Escape from the Asylum

Jordan Grupe

Manor House

Escape from the Asylum / Jordan Grupe

Library and Archives Canada
Cataloguing in Publication

Title: Escape from the asylum / Jordan Grupe.
Names: Grupe, Jordan, author.
Identifiers: Canadiana 20220427615 |
ISBN 9781988058863 (softcover) |
ISBN 9781988058870 (hardcover)
Subjects: LCGFT: Novels.
Classification: LCC PS8613.R88 E83 2022 | DDC C813/.6—dc23
Note: This novel is a work of fiction. Any resemblance to locations or persons alive or dead is purely coincidental.

First Edition
Cover Design-layout / Interior- layout: Michael Davie, J. Grupe
Cover image: Canva.com
192 pages / 55.266 words. All rights reserved.
Published October 2022 / Copyright 2022
Manor House Publishing Inc.
452 Cottingham Crescent, Ancaster, ON, L9G 3V6
www.manor-house-publishing.com (905) 648-4797

Description: Detective Franklin Reynard awakes one morning to find his partner missing and a murderer is on the loose. The suspect is an escaped mental patient with a violent history, who has vanished, taking a young boy with her as a hostage. As the mystery deepens, Reynard is drawn into a terrifying labyrinth of darkness beneath the local asylum. Something tells him the answer he seeks lies beneath the infamous 150-year-old mental hospital, but he'll need help to uncover the answers. This thriller expands on Beneath the Asylum - the first novel by Jordan Grupe.

This project has been made possible [in part] by the Government of Canada. « *Ce projet a été rendu possible [en partie] grâce au gouvernement du Canada.*

Funded by the Government of Canada
Financé par le gouvernement du Canada

Canada

Escape from the Asylum / Jordan Grupe

*For Berndt,
Miss you, Dad*

Acknowledgements

Thank you to my mom, Vanessa for her help with editing and advice on this novel and my other books. I can't tell you how much I appreciate you for all that you do. You're an amazing person and you've taught me so much.

Dad, we'll catch up at the nineteenth hole. I miss you every day.

Thank you to my wife, Chloe. You help me to look at the world in a different lens and you make me a better person. You inspire me every day and I love you so much.

My sincere gratitude to Mike Davie for publishing this book and others. You are fulfilling a lifelong dream of seeing my work published and I can't thank you enough for taking a chance on this upstart internet writer. Thank you also to Ryan Davie and the rest of the family.

Thanks also to Nolan, my brother. When I write you're almost always my imaginary reader. You did what all good older brothers do, you showed me the good shit. Kurt Vonnegut, Joe Hill, Nick Cutter, etc. Thanks for having great taste. Hope you liked this one too. Thank you to all my friends and family as well for supporting me in my writing and in everything else I do. I love you all.

And finally, my thanks to you, the reader. If not for you this book would not exist. To everyone who follows my work on Reddit, Amazon, and YouTube – you have my sincere gratitude. I never imagined that people would seek out my work and would want to read my stories, and it really is a dream come true. I hope you enjoyed reading this strange tale as much as I enjoyed writing it.

Jordan Grupe

November 26th 2022

About the Author:

Jordan Grupe is a Hamilton, Ontario-based author and artist, who has created horror novels along with hundreds of short stories.

His writings are often shared with a vast audience in the millions via the websites Reddit.com (under profile Jgrupe) and YouTube as well as author website: JordanGrupe.com, and more.

The author and his works are also featured on an array of other websites, including amazon.com and other Amazon sites; the websites of other major books retailers and the publisher's website, manor-house-publishing.com.

Escape from the Asylum is the author's second novel and third book, following his best-selling horror novel **Beneath the Asylum** and his breakthrough collection of horror short stories *No Sleep Tonight*.

Although *Escape from the Asylum* is a work of fiction, it draws its inspiration from the author's own experience as a security guard at a psychiatric hospital with a dilapidated, and reportedly haunted, old mansion on its grounds.

Praise for *Escape from the Asylum*:

Jordan Grupe once again drags readers into a vivid nightmare where there is no way out with his second novel, *Escape from the Asylum*. If you've ever wondered what it would be like to be trapped in a haunted mental asylum--first of all, *what is wrong with you?*--and second, Grupe's got the answer. *Escape* will have you hiding under the covers with a flashlight too scared to keep reading but even more afraid to stop. Don't sleep on this book because, after reading it, you might never sleep again."
-**Travis Brown**, author, *House with 100 Doors*

"From Jordan Grupe, author of the dark masterpiece *Beneath the Asylum,* comes his equally disturbing sequel *Escape from the Asylum* in which the destroyed mental institution "springs up like a poisonous mushroom," restoring its sinister presence just as all memories – even news stories – of its prior existence are erased. It's an insane, twisted trip down memory lane no one in their right mind would ever willingly take. This time, the dangers are more intense, the implications more macabre and the return visit more gut-wrenching – is there any way of stopping this horrifying history from repeating itself with even more tragic results?"
- **Michael B, Davie**, author, *The Late Man*

"Jordan Grupe weaves magic with his horror, building a world of nightmares that steals your attention and refuses to let go. Escape from the Asylum is more than just a good read - it's an unforgettable one."
- **Jason Martin**, author, *Crooked Antlers*

"Jordan Grupe is a master horror teller firing on all cylinders."
Marcus Starr, Author, *Nora's Curse.*

Prologue

Well, That's a Bit Strange, Don't You Think?

The two security guards stood facing the old manor at the back of the mental hospital grounds. A casual passerby might have thought that they were admiring it, standing alone before it as they were, staring up at the dilapidated building. But they were not admiring it.

The guard on the right, blonde-haired and rail-thin, let out a soft whistle. There had been a long period of silence between the two young men.

"Well, you're right. It's back. From the ashes - reborn."

"Don't say it like that."

"How else am I supposed to say it? I mean, it's not just me, right? This is fucking weird, isn't it?"

"You mean a century and a half old building that was burnt to the ground suddenly standing there as if nothing ever happened? Yeah, especially considering the building we're talking about, it's weird."

They stood in silence for a few moments longer.

"Well, the timing of it doesn't help anything," the guard on the left said. He was taller than the other guard, a bit heavier-set with short brown hair.

"Just before I'm about to go on leave and you're heading off on paternity - this thing springs up like a poisonous mushroom."

"Yeah," the blonde-haired guard agreed. "It's a bad omen, that's for sure, if nothing else. It was *her* favourite place, after all. And the door at the west end of the basement has been awfully quiet lately."

"She's going back to her old stomping grounds. Century Manor. Her *Happy Place.*"

They were both quiet again and then the tall guard spoke once more.

"Well, we knew she was powerful. I didn't realize she was *this* powerful, though. You wanna know what the worst part of all this is?"

"What's that?"

"Nobody else remembers this building burnt down. Just us. I've asked around. And all the news articles and references to it online are gone too, like it never happened. Like none of it ever happened. Everything we accomplished - it's like we never did any of it."

"What the fuck? Are you sure?"

"Yeah, and not only that…"

The old manor's front door suddenly swung open, creaking loudly in the night. Pure blackness, as dark as the lowest point of the ocean, or the deepest tunnel underground, peeked out from inside. The dusty old building's features could barely be made out at the entrance - old rotting wood, moldy tapestries, dusty chandeliers, and a multitude of spider webs. As if it had been there for a hundred and fifty years uninterrupted.

"Are you gonna close that?" the tall guard asked the other. "Some kid could wander in there."

"Can't you close it?"

"Aw hell no, c'mon man, you're the supervisor."

"Exactly, and you're my subordinate, right? So, you close it."

"Nuh uh. You owe me one. I saved your life, remember?"

"After I saved yours! Twice!"

"Oh, fine. But we're even now."

The guard's face went a shade paler and he sighed resignedly. He took a hesitant step forward, and then another.

Just as he reached the stairs, the door swung open wide as if blown by a gust of wind from inside the house. Rancid-smelling air rushed out, like the reek of corpse-flesh and decay, straining the door on its hinges, banging against the porch railing outside.

The security guard stumbled backwards, falling to the ground as he screamed. It felt like there was a hurricane brewing inside the house and they had just let it out.

And then the door slammed shut again. It was completely silent except for the rapid sound of their breathing.

Both of the guards recovered for a minute and then slowly began to walk away, taking uneasy glances over their shoulders as they did.

"Well, it's somebody else's problem now. We'll just have to deal with her somehow when we get back. How bad could things get? We're only gonna be off for a year or so."

Their voices faded away in the distance and as they did another sound came into focus. The thing that was once a girl named Samantha waited and listened as the source of it came into view.

It was a tall doctor, elderly with dark hair. He strode quickly with a suitcase in hand, walking towards a black BMW. As he did, he passed by the front of the old manor. He did not usually think about it - the mansion had been there twice as long as he had been alive. But today he slowed down and looked at the building with an odd admiration, like he had never felt before. Something about it was calling to him.

One day soon it will be torn down to make room for condos, with the way things are headed, he thought to himself. *A shame, really. It's a monument to those old, early days of psychiatry. Back when it was an exciting, burgeoning field of study with grand experiments and untested hypotheses. Not like today...*

Just as he was going past the front of the building, he heard a sound.

The front door of the old house opened on its hinges, as if by someone unseen. He stopped and looked. Inside was only darkness. It was getting late in the day and the sun was going down. The doctor looked at his wristwatch and sighed.

"Hello," he called out. "If this is a prank of some sort I'm not in the mood."

"Hello," a young girl's voice called back softly, sounding afraid. "Can you help me please?"

The doctor set down his briefcase.

"Are you alright? Why don't you come out here so I can see you? We can call your parents to pick you up if you're lost. It's okay, you won't be in any trouble."

The voice sounded like it was struggling in the darkness of the house.

"I can't. It's my foot - it got stuck under this loose board. My friends were with me but they ran off without me and... I'm scared! Help me, please!"

With an annoyed shake of his head, the doctor began to climb the front steps of the old house, leaving his briefcase outside. He walked up the stairs hesitantly, feeling a tingling sensation on the back of his neck, as if being watched.

He pushed the door open wider.

"Where are you? I can't see you," he called out.

"Down here, in the basement," the voice called back, quieter now, more distant. "Help me, please, it hurts! My foot hurts so bad."

The doctor took a tentative step inside, and then another.

As soon as he was clear of the door, it slammed shut behind him, and all was silent again in the shadow of Century Manor...

Escape from the Asylum / Jordan Grupe

1: Birds of a Feather Flock Together

The hospital foyer smelled like a slaughterhouse.

One wall was red with bloody handprints - there were streaks on the glass door and splashes of it on the ceiling, on the floor, and surrounding the body of a dead security guard in a coagulated pool.

"How could someone do something like this?" Detective Reynard asked the uniformed officer standing next to him.

"I don't know... I've never fully understood it - that's probably why I could never work in a place like this."

"Sure. But I mean literally, how could somebody do this without access to a weapon?"

"Ah. That I really don't know. Their fingernails? Their teeth?"

"Uh huh. Resourceful, whoever it was. And ruthless. A patient?"

"Certainly seems to be shaping up that way. Can you imagine a sane person doing this? And here I thought they were medicated to avoid these types of incidents."

The face of the security guard was unrecognizable. Both eyes had been gouged inwards with sharp fingernails - punctured and oozing now-dry ocular fluid. The carotid had been torn into like a wild animal had attacked the man. Teeth marks and scratches were all over his forearms and his hands - defensive wounds. One of his ears was missing with no trace of it anywhere and blood puddled around his head on the linoleum floor. The area had been sealed off with caution tape, as had the walkway and parking lot outside.

Crime scene analysts were inspecting the scene as well, taking photographs and collecting DNA evidence, which they swabbed from various places with Q-tips before dropping them into sealed plastic bags. Little yellow markers had been set up here and there like tiny *Wet Floor* signs left by miniature janitors. Splatters of blood and other evidence - all labelled with numbers to indicate their order for filing purposes.

"It doesn't make sense to me either. Imagine somebody doing something like this with their bare hands... You'd have to be desperate."

"We've got some cameras, I'm assuming," Reynard pointed up at the corner of the room where a tinted glass dome was mounted.

"Yeah, they're pulling it up for us now in the main office. I told them we'd head over in a minute."

Detective Reynard looked at his watch.

"Where the hell is he? It's not like him to be late like this."

"I don't know, we've called him three times. Should we send over a car?"

"Yeah, do it. Wake the old bastard up. I've seen enough here for now. Let's go check the tape."

He stood up and they left the crime scene together. Sergeant Burns had worked homicide for ten years and was a capable assistant for the time being, but he missed his partner. The nearly-retired detective was rough around the edges, prickly as a cactus this time of the morning as a general rule, but he needed all the help he could get on this one.

The two of them went up a short flight of stairs and walked up a corridor towards the main office where a uniformed security guard was waiting for them. He led them through a series of locked doors into a switchboard area, then past that into another room marked "Security Office."

"We've got it cued up for you. I managed to find something on camera 32. It shows a view of the section H foyer where it all happened. We're combing through the other cameras too, trying to see if we can find anything - we'll save the data as well so it won't be overwritten."

"I'll need a copy of this and all the other cameras if you can manage it. The last twenty four hours."

"Yeah, we can make that happen. Whatever we can do to help you catch this... woman."

Reynard got the impression that wouldn't have been his first choice of words if he weren't trying admirably to maintain his professionalism. The guard moved the video forward in time until it showed a security guard coming inside through the double glass doors. He turned around to close them behind him and then checked to make sure they were locked, giving them a swift tug.

Burns jumped. A woman could be seen moving in from the shadows - her footsteps appeared careful, deliberate, and predatory. The guard on the video had no time to react. Within moments he was bleeding and desperately thrashing and kicking at the air as she held him from behind and tore at his throat with her teeth, blood squirting into the air and jetting out from his artery like a burst water main. First attacking him like a wild animal, the woman then proceeded to take him to the ground with surprising force. She tore off his ear with her teeth and put it calmly into her front shirt pocket.

The woman grabbed keys from his pocket, wiped the blood from her mouth with her sleeve, then left through the glass double doors, fleeing to the parking lot where she stole the guard's car, presumably locating it with the automatic key fob.

"Who is she?"

The security guard pulled out a file folder and opened it, revealing a document with patient records and a glossy photo. The woman in the photo had a tattoo on her forehead, crudely etched with blue ink - large block capital letters reading the word *BETRAYED* were stamped above her eyes. Her hair was long and dirty blonde and she had eyes the colour of swamp water. A thin face showed lines around the mouth and under her eyes - hints of age.

Only a psychopath would get a tattoo like that, he thought to himself. *That's the face of a murderer if I've ever seen one.*

"Gertrude Remier - arrested for assaulting her sister, badly injuring her - found *innocent* by reason of insanity. She was being held in the Forensics Unit on E2. It's a locked ward - the patients there are involuntary committals, brought in from jail still wearing the shackles and orange jumpsuits. But then once they're here they take the shackles off and they medicate them, they do group sessions, talk therapy, rec-time. Within a month the ones who do well begin to be allowed outside unsupervised. Most do alright and come back, but others hop on the bus and we have to call you guys to bring 'em back."

"I remember from when I used to work patrol, way back when. So you're saying she absconded? When was that?"

"She'd been allowed out that afternoon and then never came back to the ward. We put in a report with you guys - but I guess one hand doesn't always talk to the other. My guess... Looking back, I don't think she ever left the hospital grounds."

"How the hell is that possible?" he asked, slightly annoyed. "You're saying she was hiding around here in plain sight and nobody noticed her?"

Now it was the guard's turn to get defensive.

"Hey, we've only got two or three guards on at a time when we're short-staffed, which these days we usually are. One of those guards is stuck in a booth outside E2, doing access control, and they can't move from that station. Throw in the fact that this property is twenty acres, and you're damn right we didn't notice her! We were on the lookout for her - sure. Same as we were on the lookout for five or six other patients. But there's plenty of places to hide around here.

"I'd guess she was in the basement, though, hiding down in one of those old tunnels. Then, when it was quiet, she came up to the main level and hid under the steps right there," he pointed at the screen, indicating a shadowy corner. "And waited for somebody to come along by themselves with a set of keys."

Reynard nodded.

"Show me these tunnels down in the basement."

The lower level of the hospital was just as creepy as the rumors around town would have people believe. Reynard couldn't help but feel a bit relieved when he heard the voice of someone calling for him from down the hallway, near the elevator.

"Reynard, phone call for you upstairs!"

He was inspecting a lock in a dark old side tunnel which was full of spider webs and not much else. The air was cold, musty, and wet. A few scratches indicated damage from someone's attempts to pick the keyhole. They weren't an expert, whoever they were - at least not at lockpicking. Still, it appeared they had succeeded. The door hung open by half a foot. It was nothing conclusive, but it was something at least.

"Tell them to call back, I'm busy."

"They said it's an emergency! Something about your partner."

That got his attention. He pulled out his cell phone and saw the *No Service* warning at the top. No wonder they were going through the hospital switchboard to reach him. The thick concrete walls surrounding him were allowing no transmissions in or out.

He went back up the dark tunnel towards the elevator, his flashlight bouncing in time with his hurried steps. Hustling towards the exit, he felt eyes watching him from the darkness, a tingling sensation on his neck. Surely just his imagination, but he looked back just the same.

As he looked over his shoulder, he tripped and nearly fell over a pipe. Reynard picked himself up and kept moving. There was a sinking feeling in his stomach that he didn't like one bit, and it got worse with every moment he spent in this basement.

Escape from the Asylum / Jordan Grupe

"It's Jim! Something's happened at his place, you've got to get over there now," the semi-hysterical voice on the phone was totally unlike the normally calm, rational voice of Delores, the dispatch operator.

Reynard didn't waste any time, the sinking feeling in his gut solidifying into a dreadful knot like a heavy cinder block of guilt. He should have gone over there himself after his partner neglected to show up for duty at the crime scene that morning. Such behaviour was totally unlike him, and explained the unease that permeated his day so far - accentuated by the dark grey clouds, which blanketed the sky. A stress headache was forming beneath his forehead like a bad knee aching with the premonition of foul weather. Just as he had that thought it began to patter down in fat drops which landed heavily on his head and his hands while he ran through the parking lot towards his battered black sedan.

He climbed into the Crown Victoria and backed out of the spot, peeling away and leaving a grey plume in the air behind him, matching the clouds. The drive towards his partner's house was full of strange thoughts, but one foremost in his mind - the photograph of the escaped patient. She had looked familiar for some reason, and furthermore he associated her with his partner. But he couldn't understand for the life of him why.

When she opened the door he understood immediately.

Detective Reynard actually reached for his gun at first, before understanding it all in one instant. His hand relaxed and her face betrayed no hint of noticing his near-fatal error. "She's your sister," he said, the words slipping out of his mouth before he could stop himself.

The woman standing before him crumpled and her face looked suddenly destroyed with anguish as she fell into him, sobbing. She clutched the lapels of his suit, gripping them in white-knuckled misery.

"So it's true. It is her! I knew it had to be her! She took Greg and I think she killed Jim!"

Escape from the Asylum / Jordan Grupe

The scene at Jim's house made even Reynard feel slightly nauseated. Maybe it was the coppery tang of blood in the air, twice in one morning in two different places, or perhaps the fact that this crime scene was his partner's house, not some stranger who he could disassociate from. He wasn't callous, not by any stretch, but his occupation required a certain level of detachment to get the job done.

Not just detachment, he thought. *It's more than that. I have to imagine I'm the twisted fuck who does these things - I have to put myself in their shoes. But how do I do that when they killed my best friend? How do I pretend to be someone who I despise?*

Remain objective. Don't let your senses get fooled by your emotions.

Still, it was difficult. The lack of a corpse only made it more so. He winced at that observation as soon as he had made it.

A part of him wanted to run out to his car and go look for his partner. But he knew there were others out doing that. His job was to stay here and inspect the scene - to see the things that others had missed - and yet he felt as if he were floating underwater in a dream. The whole thing felt surreal and he just wished he could wake up from this nightmare.

Jim was the guy he played cards with twice a month. Jim was the man who had helped him through his wife's death and who had helped to keep him from wallowing in the depths of a depression that he hadn't even realized the full extent of until much later, when he was starting to see his way out of it.

But what Jim was not, what he was never supposed to be - at least in Reynard's mind - was a victim. The two identifiers were polar opposites. Jim was the one who helped the victims, who caught the bad guys. He was one of the best at it. The man was a bulldog. A six foot five bruiser with wide shoulders who took shit from no one and gave it back double if you tried.

Escape from the Asylum / Jordan Grupe

And now where was he? Bleeding out in a back alley somewhere? Or in the trunk of that bitch's car, dying as she made her way towards the back roads and out of town?

A smaller CSI team had arrived to explore this new crime scene - their resources now divided in half between the two. More roadblocks had been set up, more agencies called in. More tiny, numbered pieces of folded plastic were set up next to congealed pools of blood.

Pictures were taken, measurements were made, and samples of everything were swabbed and stored for analysis.

Blood was spotted in various places throughout the main floor of the home, and at the door, but primarily it was in the kitchen where a large quantity had been spilled. To Reynard's trained eyes, he could see plainly the signs of a struggle. The coffee maker was tipped onto the floor, the carafe broken and covered in still-fresh blood.

Lieutenant Snead entered the kitchen as Reynard was examining another mark of blood on a door frame.

"She's not far. Wherever she is. But I don't know about Jim. Unless she had help I can't see her getting him into the car's trunk. There's no sign of someone being dragged and either way somebody would have seen something. But there is a handprint near the door and I'll bet it's Jim's. I think he got out. I think Jim ran after whatever happened here. Maybe for help - but I don't think so. I can't see him abandoning his family, it just doesn't make any fucking sense. Can you picture him running from this?"

"No. But people do shit they normally wouldn't do when their body goes into survival mode. Fight or flight, remember? All that. We've got the dogs working on it. They'll find him."

"Why the hell did she take the kid? That's what I want to know," Reynard lowered his voice slightly, "And how the *fuck* did *Allison* not hear this all happening?"

Escape from the Asylum / Jordan Grupe

"First thing I asked her."

The Lieutenant had just been talking with Jim's wife at the station for the last hour.

"She was in the shower, then blow drying her hair. She was expecting him to be gone for work by the time she got out of the tub, but instead she found this."

"You believe her?"

"Normally, no. We both know damn well how husbands and wives like to kill each other. That's your number one suspect every time in a case like this. That goes without saying. But you combine everything here with the scene at the hospital, our suspect, their history... You can't deny she looks good for this one too. The sister, I mean. She's responsible for both, there's no way she's not."

Reynard thought about that for a few moments.

"It just seems odd," Reynard said at length. "She kills the guard at the hospital, takes his car, then comes back here, kills Jim, or at least wounds him real bad, we don't know, but that's a whole hell of a lot of blood and it must have come from somebody, right? And then she takes their son and leaves?"

"You're the one who's so good at getting into these sick fucks' heads - you tell me. Does she want her to suffer mentally like she did? Is that it? Psychological warfare?"

The Lieutenant had worked homicide for a long time, but he was right - Reynard was better at this part of it than he was. Better than Jim or anyone else on the force, too. He'd always found a way to get into the mind of the killer. To see it from their perspective. And what the Lieutenant said should have made sense, but it didn't sit right with Reynard. None of this did.

"We need to make sure she's got police protection once she's out of the station."

Escape from the Asylum / Jordan Grupe

"Already done. She'll have a uniformed officer with her 24/7 after we're finished talking with her. Gertrude wants revenge and it isn't going to stop at this, I'll bet you anything. Now, do you see something here with those eagle eyes of yours?"

"I see a crime scene that doesn't make any damn sense, that's what I see. She could have had help, I guess. Carried him out with another person. We're gonna need to wait for some lab results to come back. I need to know who this blood belongs to. All of it."

Another man entered the room wearing a tan trench coat, his hair slick from the rain. He stood awkwardly at the doorway as if waiting to be invited into the blood-filled kitchen.

"Who the hell is this?" Reynard asked, hooking his thumb in the newcomer's direction.

"Dell Burton, meet your new mentor."

The guy stuck out his hand for Reynard to shake. He ignored it.

"He's your partner, Reynard, at least for the time being. I can't have you working alone on this, you know that."

"Oh, you gotta be kidding. What is he, twelve? The kid looks fresh outta the fucking academy. Don't do me dirty like this, Snead."

To his credit, the kid's expression never changed, showing no hint of embarrassment or resentment. He simply stood there watching the show.

"He's new to us but he's an asset. Use him as such. You might be surprised what the kid is capable of."

With that, he walked out, clapping the kid on the shoulder as he left.

"You boys catch this psycho bitch, alright? Don't fuck this up. I'm gonna go make a statement to the press. God help me."

He left them alone in the blood-covered room.

"How'd you get this assignment, anyways?" Reynard asked, turning the Crown Victoria onto the street. "This is high-profile shit. How'd you get pegged as the newbie?"

"I've got some experience - guess they thought I'd be a good fit."

"Where did you work before this, kid?"

"Military Police. I served four years in Afghanistan. Got back and wanted to keep doing the same thing I was doing over there - I loved the job. Most days, anyways. Sorry about your partner."

"Don't say you're sorry. We don't know if there's anything to be sorry about yet."

Only that there was a helluva lot of blood back there. People don't survive after losing that much blood, you know that.

The kid's eyes told Reynard he'd lost more than one friend himself. Maybe he'd be helpful after all. Once again he was reminded not to judge a book by its cover.

"An MP, huh? You ever have to solve a big case over there in Afghanistan?"

"Yeah, once. Infantry soldier sexually assaulted by a superior. All the other members of the squad said they didn't hear anything, nobody wanted to say shit about who was responsible. But we figured it out after a day or two. It went to trial, the guy went to jail. Hopefully he rots there."

"So you caught him? Good job."

"Didn't feel like it. All the other guys who refused to talk - they got the word out that I was going after my own. That I wasn't to be trusted. They said the perp was a stand-up guy and I was just trying to further my career. I did get a promotion, but nobody at base looked at me the same after that. I was a pariah, according to them. That's part of the reason I never reenlisted. I couldn't stand looking at their faces anymore."

"Damn. Well, good for you. You did the right thing."

"Yeah, I know. So, where we headed next?"

"Back to the hospital. I want to talk to the staff and the patients, anybody who knows Gertrude personally."

An Amber Alert had been issued already and the police were on the lookout for a vehicle matching the description of the one Gertrude was presumed to be driving.

The car she had stolen from the security guard was a late-model light blue Honda Civic - sadly one of the more common vehicles on the road. This would make it tricky for police to find it, but roadblocks had been set up on all major thoroughfares leading out of town.

The noose was tightening, and Gertrude would have to be extremely clever to escape the area without being noticed.

"Sounds like a plan," said Dell, drumming his fingers with anticipation. "Most people can't keep a secret. Hopefully she let something slip about what she had planned to a friend. Maybe someone there can tell us something."

Despite the words, Reynard could tell that Dell had little hope in this expedition yielding results. In fact, neither did he. But he found it always helped to talk to as many witnesses as possible before starting down any road of an investigation.

People were unreliable, but they often gave tidbits of useful information - breadcrumbs which led down a path into a dark forest.

A place he knew all too well.

2: A Trip Down Memory Lane

"She never talked much to any of us," said the young nurse sitting in front of Reynard. "But to the doctors she did. And in group sessions she would say just enough to get by, so that we didn't single her out for not participating, I think. In retrospect I'm pretty sure I was right about my suspicions. Everything she did was just to build up trust so she could get privileges. We've seen it before. It's no secret around here that if you go with the program you start to get your life back, a little bit at a time."

"Meaning?"

"Meaning she was allowed to go outside for a cigarette, to go down to the cafeteria. This isn't a prison, it's a hospital, we never pretend that's not the case. And when you're a patient in a hospital you have certain rights - under the Patients' Rights Act. You follow the rules, show progress, you begin to get your rights back, one by one, bit by bit. We even trusted her enough to leave for the day once to visit her family, under their supervision, of course."

"Whose supervision specifically?"

"Her sister, Allison, I believe her name is."

"Twins, right?"

"Yes, that's right. Identical if not for that disgusting tattoo. Sorry, I shouldn't judge, but it just shows what state of mind she's in. Paranoid, unrepentant, blaming everyone but herself for her mistakes."

"So she left around what time?"

"It was three o'clock I would guess, right around there. You can check the sign-out sheet to see exactly. But that was her usual time. Anyways she was supposed to come back for dinner. Obviously that never happened."

"She have any friends? People she would have talked to about this?"

The nurse looked at the ceiling and thought about this for a little while. He could tell she was really trying, but the look on her face told him mostly what he needed to know.

"Not really, to be honest. Maybe a word or two here and there at meals. In session, like I said, she opened up a bit. But then whenever I saw her in the halls or in the lounge, she'd be quiet. Even if there were other people around she wouldn't talk to them unless they spoke to her first. And then it would be quick one word answers - she never really made friends with anyone."

"What about the staff? Any nurses she was partial to? Or doctors who she talked with openly?"

"Well, that's another story. You can talk to Sarah. She did one to one with her a lot right after she came in."

"One to one?" Dell asked. "Sorry, what's that?"

"When we get worried somebody might do something - hurt someone or hurt themselves - we get somebody to sit with them. Twenty four hours a day."

"Yeah? So she was not to be trusted? I thought she was a model patient the way you said she got privileges to leave the unit so quickly..."

"Model patient? No, not her. Matthew over there - he's a model patient," she pointed out the window of the small office in the direction of a chubby man with glasses who appeared to be in his twenties.

Escape from the Asylum / Jordan Grupe

"Matthew does everything we expect from a patient. He participates in group talk, eats all his meals, comes back on time from his afternoon pass. She was never really like that. She went with the program to a certain extent, sure, but you could tell that she resented all of us. She only did what she was told so she would get what she wanted."

"And what was that exactly?"

The nurse looked at the two of them like it was the most obvious thing in the world.

"Freedom."

Sarah was a tall, rail-thin girl with braces and long mousy brown hair that appeared frizzy and slightly damp, held up in bright pink butterfly clips.

"So you're a nurse here on E2?" Reynard asked.

"Personal Support Worker," she said cheerily, breaking into a pimple-faced smile which revealed pink rubber bands in her dental equipment, matching her hair clips. "I'm still in nursing school. Two more years to go."

Her speech was slightly strained and saliva-sounding through the braces and he wondered if they were new and she was still getting used to them.

"Ah, I see. And do you want to keep working here once you're certified? Or are you looking to switch it up after all this?"

She opened her mouth to say something and at that second Reynard's phone began to ring. He excused himself and went to stand outside the small meeting room to answer the call.

"We've got her. At a gas station on Highway six. She was just there filling up the dead guard's Honda. Ten minutes ago, maybe less."

"I'm on my way."

Escape from the Asylum / Jordan Grupe

3: A Friend in Need is a Friend Indeed

The gas station was an old one with pumps that didn't take cards. You had to walk inside to pay the man behind the counter. Or in this case, the pimple-faced teenager.

"She looked nuts, man. Had this big fucking tattoo stamped on her forehead. 'Betrayed!' Like she's the fuckin' Terminator or some shit..."

"Did you see if there was anybody else in the car with her? It's important if you saw anybody with her."

The kid's reddened eyes looked thoughtful for a few moments but then he looked away, uncertain.

"Maybe. I... I looked out there and I *think* maybe I saw somebody moving around in the back seat. But I'm not sure. Could have been, though."

"A kid? A young boy, maybe?"

"Yeah, could've been. Like I said, I'm not a hundred percent."

You'd probably remember better if you could lay off the weed for five minutes, Reynard thought to himself. The smell of it was wafting off the kid like he had it hanging to dry in the back room. Maybe he did. It wasn't like this was a reputable establishment, just an old run down gas station on a one-lane country road.

Dell, his new partner, was in the back room with the manager of the place looking at the security camera footage.

Suddenly Reynard's phone began to ring. It said *Unknown Number* on the screen and he hesitated before picking it up. The spam calls were getting to be damn-near constant recently. The day prior he'd received *thirty five calls* from various numbers, often back to back within a few minutes of each other. When he answered one it had been a recorded message playing in Mandarin. After that they had become nearly constant. He would have to change his phone number again.

Still, something was telling him he should pick up this mystery call. He wasn't sure why, but he had a strong feeling in his gut telling him to answer. His mind imagined him answering and Gertrude being on the other end of the line, Jim's son Greg screaming in the background.

Stepping outside the gas station, he hit the *accept* button.

"Reynard here," he said, holding his breath afterwards.

A wet cough came through the ear piece. The breathing on the other end sounded labored and rattled in and out.

"Listen. It's not…" the voice began, then broke off in a horrible coughing fit.

"Jim!?"

"Hhhrrkk, listen… Not much time… can't…"

"Jim?? Where are you? I'll come get you, just tell me where you are!"

"…Gertrude. It wasn't… HER, Reynard. Tell my son. And tell him I love him."

The voice was impossible to hear, the whispered sound of it dying in his ear.

"JIM! JIM!? ARE YOU STILL THERE? Where are you?"

Nothing.

He kept the line open before calling into the station. Once they picked up he told them to trace the call and dispatch police and EMS to the location.

Escape from the Asylum / Jordan Grupe

A couple minutes later, he had an address.

Dell came out of the gas station shaking his head. The only footage they had from the security camera was of Gertrude pumping her gas and then entering the store. It was definitely her - the tattoo stamped on her forehead left no question. There was only one person in the world with a tattoo like that and it made identification very simple.

"We gotta go. They located Jim's phone. He just called me."

"What about Gertrude? She's gotta be close."

"We've got every cop in the city looking for her. Our job is to figure out what the hell happened."

"Alright, I'm taking your lead on this."

They jumped in the black Crown Victoria and sped off down the country road. The engine roared as Reynard pushed down on the gas, screaming towards town with the siren blazing.

They located Jim at a payphone in a parking lot, his body slumped in a phone booth and no longer breathing. His shirt was drenched in blood and so were his hands and arms. The defensive wounds Reynard had noted on the security guard were present here as well - hands split open in places where it appeared a knife had struck.

EMS arrived and checked his pulse, pronouncing him dead on the scene. The area was cordoned off, and after the police tape had been strung around the perimeter he had a few moments to survey the scene. His second dead body that day - and it wasn't even noon.

"Were you guys close?" Dell asked from behind.

"We were partners. For the last five years we were together every day. We played cards every other weekend." Reynard took a deep, shuddering breath, tilting his head upwards to dry the tears forming in his eyes, hoping no one would notice them. "Yeah, we were close."

The sound of camera shutters filled the early morning, their bright flashes blinding, disorienting him as he stalked away from his partner's corpse. People stood on their front steps, watching the scene unfold from across the street.

"I'm gonna go talk to those people, see if they saw anything."

"I'll come with you," said Dell.

They walked across the street together and the man standing there could be seen shuffling on his feet and looking slightly nervous.

Interesting, thought Reynard, who could easily sense the anxiety even from a hundred yards away. *I wonder what he's so nervous about.*

"Morning, officers," the man said as they approached. He swallowed and again glanced over his shoulder into the house behind him.

"Good morning. Mind if we come in to talk with you for a minute?"

The man turned a shade paler.

"Place is a mess right now," he said. "How about we talk out here."

"Sure. No problem. Did you see what happened here this morning? We're just checking if anyone witnessed anything that could help with the investigation."

"Nope, sorry. Just saw the flashing lights and stepped outside to see what was going on. Who was he? Drug dealer or something?"

Reynard felt his back go up at the suggestion, especially after his partner had just died violently, he was ready to defend his honor. But he reminded himself to stay calm. The investigation was what was important.

"See anybody coming or going?" he asked, ignoring the man's question. "Anyone at all?"

"Just you guys. Like I said, I saw the flashing lights and came out to look. Not sure exactly what happened."

"Okay, I understand. How about leading up to this, in the past few days, weeks? Any suspicious activity or people in the area? Anything you can tell us that might be of use, we'd greatly appreciate it."

The guy thought about this again for a few moments then said something very strange.

"I mean, there was that tall guy."

"Tall guy?"

The man's face reddened and he looked at his feet for a few seconds before continuing.

"Yeah. It's probably nothing. Forget about it."

"No, please. Tell me about the 'tall guy.'"

"I wouldn't have noticed him except he parks in the same spot every night. Right over there," he said, pointing a few blocks down. "He just sits there with his lights off. I was out walking the dog two nights ago and I noticed him again sittin' there. Looking like he's waiting for somebody."

"Do you remember when you first saw him? How often are we talking about that you see him sitting out there?"

"Three or four times this week, at least. Can't remember when he first started showing up, but it's been more and more often lately. He just sits there most of the time then I'll look outside again and he's gone. Never stays for more than an hour or so."

"You remember what type of vehicle it was? The colour or the make and model?"

"Black. BMW, I think. Yeah, I'm pretty sure it was. He's a bald guy. Older with white hair."

"Bald *with* white hair? How can you have white hair if you're bald?"

"Ever see *Curb Your Enthusiasm?*"

"No, what the hell is that? A television show?"

The guy pulled out his cell phone and typed something into Google. Then he turned the phone around to show the screen to Reynard, revealing a thin man with glasses, balding with white hair.

"Larry David - he's the guy who co-created *Seinfeld*. See his head? Bald, right? What else would you call that?"

"True."

"With white hair," he repeated.

"Okay. So did he look like Larry David?"

"No. Not this guy. More sophisticated. Stuffed shirt type. Maybe some facial hair, too. I can't remember for sure but I think so. A mustache or a goatee maybe."

"Okay, that could help us out. Thanks. If you think of anything else, here's my card."

Reynard handed him his contact info. The man took it and said he'd call if he thought of anything else.

The two detectives walked back over to the crime scene. They were only a few blocks away from Jim's house - which happened to be in the direction the man had pointed. A few officers were there to canvas the area so he told them about the tall man in the black BMW. It might have been nothing - but still, you never knew. It had been significant enough that the guy had brought it up, after all.

And it wasn't just that. The man had looked frightened when he'd talked about the tall man with the white hair. Spooked, as if talking about a ghost.

Reynard underlined the notation he had made which read: *Tall man, balding, white hair - Black BMW.*

Then he put a star next to it and circled it. He had a feeling it was going to be important.

"Okay, let's talk about the timeline," Reynard said once they were back in the car. "We've got a dead guard at St. Daniel's Mental Hospital. The timestamp on the video puts that murder at 0430. The body is found an hour later - a nurse going out for an early morning cigarette finds it on her way outside - so now we're at 0530. At 0700 we're over at the hospital doing our investigation when we find out that there's been a violent crime at the escaped patient's sister's house. Jim's house. Looks like she took the dead guard's car and perhaps went straight there. The sister's five year old son goes missing and her husband is nowhere to be found by the time we arrive. All we find is a lot of blood in the kitchen and all over the house.

"We get the call that someone fitting Gertrude's description is spotted at the gas station on Highway six at 0800 hours. The tattoo on her forehead makes it pretty difficult for this to be a case of mistaken identity - so we can safely say she was there only twenty minutes ago. Am I missing anything?"

He tried to be intentionally objective, ignoring all reference to the fact that his long-time partner had been a victim of murder in this particular crime.

"Yeah, that sounds right," Dell said, glancing through his notebook. "So what exactly did he say to you when he called?"

"It was hard to make it out. I could barely understand what he was saying - he was in really bad shape."

The lie came out so easily that Reynard didn't even have time to think about it.

"Hmm, okay. We'll have to get analytics to pull up the call. It should be recorded, no?"

All calls in or out of the Police Service were recorded in case they needed to be used as evidence. But he had kept it vague enough that it could be believed he hadn't heard Jim's exact words. They had been standing next to a busy highway, after all.

Reynard realized he didn't want anyone else to know yet what Jim had said. The fact that he had specifically said it wasn't Gertrude made no sense whatsoever. Of course it was her who had attacked him - there was no way around that.

"So where to now?" Dell asked him, raising his eyebrows.

It took a few moments for Reynard to realize the answer.

"The police station. I want to talk to Jim's wife, Allison."

"I thought the Lieutenant was already questioning her?"

"He is. But I have a few questions of my own."

4: Sticks and Stones

They arrived back at the police headquarters building and went up to the fourth floor where the Homicide Department was located. Reynard walked through the bullpen and found the Lieutenant in his office. Allison was no longer there.

"Where'd she go?" he asked, slightly annoyed.

"She had a helluva day. I sent her with an escort to stay in a hotel for now. We can reach her there if we need to. What the hell's the matter with you? I told you I'd fill you in on the details."

"What's wrong with me!? My partner is dead, and you send my only witness away before I can even talk to her. Who the hell is running this investigation, me or you?"

"Watch it Reynard," Lieutenant Snead said, rising from his chair. "This is my department and I'll oversee cases as I decide. You want to ask her more questions go find her at the fucking Radisson and do it yourself, nobody's stopping you. Now get out of my face. – and read the interview notes before giving me fucking attitude. They're on your desk, not that you bothered to ask."

Reynard slammed the door without another word. He felt no need to apologize or to explain himself. Snead was deviating from protocol and he couldn't understand why. Maybe just because it was such a big case, he wanted to have his name on it as part of the investigation? Either way, there was no time to think about it now.

"Man, I can't believe you get away with talking to him like that. Surprised he didn't can your ass," Reynard's new partner said.

"He knows better than that. And so should you."

He grabbed the stack of papers on his desk and practically threw them at Dell, hitting him in the gut. "Let's read it on the road."

They arrived at the hotel and found Allison's room with the assistance of the police escort who had been assigned to her. She answered the door and looked unsurprised to see them.

"Lieutenant Snead said you'd be coming. Please, come in."

There wasn't much space to sit down, aside from a chair and the bed, so Reynard stood while Dell took the chair and Allison sat on the side of the bed. She looked at them both expectantly. Her face was red from crying recently and her eyes looked dry and puffy, but she was putting up a brave front.

"I'm not sure what good I'm going to be, but I'll try to help any way I can. I'm sure you have more questions for me."

"Yes, ma'am."

"Please, Reynard, just Allison is fine. Jim talks about you a lot by the way. He adores you... *Adored* you, I should say."

She broke off into choked sobs and Reynard moved over to the bed to console her. He sat down next to her and put a hand on her shoulder.

"I'm so sorry for your loss. We both are."

She continued crying, the sobbing growing louder and louder.

"He's really gone, isn't he? They told me they found his... body..."

"Yes, I'm afraid so."

Her cries grew louder and Dell passed her a box of tissues from the bureau.

"Did he... say anything? Tell you anything that... I don't know..."

Reynard again lied. But he didn't know why. Instead of meeting her wet, hopeful eyes with his, he looked down at the floor before speaking. "No, nothing intelligible. Sorry, he was in rough shape by that point I imagine. I don't think he could say very much."

Escape from the Asylum / Jordan Grupe

But he did manage to say it wasn't Gertrude. But if it wasn't her, then who was it? She took the kid, it had to be her. There was no way around it. No way to square that circle. Unless this woman sitting beside him on the bed was lying somehow.

"They're heading north, we believe that much. Where do you think Gertrude would take Greg? If you had to take a guess?"

She looked deep in thought and he was glad to see she took the question seriously. Her answer was not at all what he expected.

"I hope she's not going to hurt him. I'm praying she won't. Still, I know she might. I need you to find him, Reynard. Find Greg. Please!"

"We're going to try our best, but what can you tell us to help? You looked like you had something in mind."

"This is going to sound ridiculous. But I think she's going to take him to our family cottage. It's the only place she knows is safe."

"Okay, that helps. Something else: Do you know about Gertrude's combat training? I see you talked with the lieutenant about her military record briefly. What can you tell me about that?"

"Well, like I told your boss, she came back from Afghanistan a completely different person. She could take care of herself, yeah. And she got into bar fights to prove it to everybody. It was like she was just so *angry* all of a sudden. I... we... all of us tried to help her... but she didn't want help. She just wanted to be angry. She shut us all out - family, friends, anyone trying to talk to her, pretended we weren't even there. And then the voices started."

"Voices?"

"Yeah. You could see her talking back to them sometimes, after a while. That was when we knew something was really going on. She'd just be sitting there on the couch and I'd be sitting beside her and I'd hear her whispering, like she was trying to talk to someone very softly. But the words would be harsh. She'd tell the voices to, 'shut up,' and, 'fuck off,' her tone so raspy and angry that it didn't even sound like her anymore."

"You say she got into a lot of fights. Did she ever lose any of them?"

Allison surprised him by giving him a tight-lipped smile. "No, detective. Gertrude never loses a fight – and never backs down." She lifted up her hair at the back to show a scar. "Not even against her own sister."

"That's quite a scar. Where did that come from?"

"A fight we had, a year ago. The one that got her locked up. I call it a fight but that's being kind to my ego. The truth is she beat me until I couldn't stand up anymore. Apparently she wasn't happy I'd been dating her ex. She smashed my head on a curb and pulled my hair until my scalp was beginning to detach, then she pulled a little more. It took six people to get her off of me."

"Where did this happen?"

"At a bar, of course. I guess it goes without saying that alcohol doesn't solve all of life's problems, it usually makes them worse. She had been holding in that rage but as soon as she got drunk she let it all out."

Something still wasn't adding up for Reynard. He had to ask the question that had been on his mind all morning.

"I'm trying to understand something. Maybe you can help me to figure it out."

"I'll try. Whatever I can do to help you find Greg."

"That's just it. Why did she take him? Why kill Jim? Why risk going into a police detective's house when you could just run?"

Allison stared at him for a few moments with no response. Her face just looked blank, emotionless.

"I don't know, detective. That you'll have to figure out for yourself."

5: Don't Count Your Chickens

Reynard hadn't eaten all day, he was starving. The kid gawked at him a bit when he pulled into the drive-through.

"Really? How can you eat at a time like this?"

"I don't operate well on an empty stomach, Dell. You want anything?"

"No, I don't want anything. I don't eat this greasy shit."

"Suit yourself."

He ordered a breakfast combo number four at the box and got an extra coffee for Dell. Eating under the contemptuous glare of his new partner, he devoured the sausage and egg sandwich in under a minute.

"That was quite a spectacle."

"Oh shut the fuck up, I was hungry. Now let's talk case."

He opened up a packet of ketchup and squirted some on the corner of his hashbrown, eating it thoughtfully.

"You're missing out, kid. I'm telling you, these hashbrowns are the best part."

"Yeah, they also give you coronary artery disease. And that ketchup is ninety percent sugar."

He rolled his eyes and took another bite, this time with a bit less ketchup. His last HBA1C had been a little high - "Pre-Diabetic" the doctor had told him. As if he needed more shit on his plate. Those words about *coronary artery disease* sounded familiar from another doctor he had seen in the past as well. It didn't help his guilty conscience that his father had died from a heart attack several years prior.

Reynard set down the rest of the hashbrown, uneaten. He had lost the rest of his appetite suddenly.

"Can we not talk about this right now? Let's talk about the fucking case already."

This new partner was not as endearing as the old curmudgeon he had known so well. Jim could power down two combo fours on his own, whereas Dell looked like he got up every morning at 5AM and did a morning jog followed by a bowl of Wheaties and a half grapefruit with no sugar. The guy was already getting on his nerves and it was just their first day together.

"What's highway patrol doing out there? I don't understand how they haven't found her yet. There's no way for her to get past those roadblocks out of town."

"Maybe she's hiding out somewhere. With a local?"

"Yeah, could be. But who does she know?"

"The sister told the lieutenant about a friend of hers who lives north of the city. Rebecca Hamstead," Dell said, reading from the thick file folder which was open on his lap.

Reynard wiped his greasy fingers off on a napkin and started the car. The big engine roared to life and the Crown Vic's undercarriage vibrated beneath their feet as it warmed up again for a moment. The days were getting colder, the nights longer. It was just after noon but time was no longer a luxury they had during the autumn season. It would be getting dark in a few hours and the possibility of her sneaking out of town became a lot more likely under cover of darkness.

"Let's go see her."

They pulled up to Rebecca Hamstead's place and found a sprawling, dirty-white, ramshackle house in the middle of a quiet country area. Kids' toys were laying out front on the lawn in disarray and a pickup truck was parked on the grass, tire tracks behind it from kicked up grass and mud. Fields lined the place on either side and the closest neighbour was a half mile away, if not more.

"Do me a favour," said Reynard. "Go around back, will you? Just to be safe. Keep a bit of distance from the house. I'll text you when I know it's her."

"What are you thinking? Gertrude might be hiding inside?"

"It's possible. My gut tells me she hasn't left the area yet. Just like at the hospital, she's hiding until dark, then she'll use the cover of night to do her dirty work. Whatever that is."

Dell agreed and went around to the back of the house, staying close to the brickwork at the side to avoid anyone looking out a window and seeing him. Meanwhile, Reynard approached the front door. He knocked and waited for someone to answer.

"Hello, can I help you?" A woman who looked to be in her sixties with greying hair answered the door. There was no hint of anxiety or worry in her eyes and Reynard relaxed a little bit.

"Hi, I'm Detective Reynard with the Hallesworth Police Department," he said, showing his badge. "May I come in? I'd like to ask you a few questions about Gertrude Renier."

Her face dropped and she stepped back a few inches from the door, eyeing him suspiciously.

"What do you want to know about her? She's locked up."

"Not anymore. She's escaped custody. There's no sense in me trying to cover it up, since the media will be running with the story by the time tonight's local news airs. She's out. Any idea where she might have gone? There's a missing kid involved and we're pretty sure she has him."

"I doubt it. Gertrude always hated children."

"That's not very reassuring at the moment, to be honest. The kid is missing and all signs indicate she took him, and she's unstable and violent."

"That's what you say. I love the bitch - we've been ride or die ever since middle school."

"Can we come in?" Reynard repeated. "I'd really like to ask you a few questions."

"You can ask them out here. I don't let strangers in my house."

"But we're police officers."

"*Especially* when they're police officers."

"Fair enough."

He didn't text Dell. It was entirely conceivable she was harboring Gertrude in her house somewhere - that would explain her reluctance to allow them entry. He decided to try something.

"You know, we could get a warrant to look inside your place. A judge would be easily convinced, especially with how you're acting right now. I don't want to have to do that - because we'll make a big mess probably if we do it that way - but we need to know where she is. If she's here, you tell me right now and you and your kids have nothing to worry about."

"My kids? Listen, I already told you. She isn't here. You go ahead and get your warrant, if you wanna waste your time. I'm done talkin' to you, asshole."

She slammed the door in his face.

"MRS. HAMSTEAD! PLEASE!"

He knocked on the door hard, hammering at it with his fist.

"SHE KILLED MY PARTNER! A MAN WITH A WIFE AND A SON! YOU MIGHT HATE THE POLICE BUT HOW CAN YOU WANT SOMEONE LIKE THAT TO GET AWAY WITH MURDER!?"

He saw her inside, through the window at the front door. She had been walking away from the front entrance but she stopped.

She turned around and looked at him through the window, then shouted loud enough for him to hear.

"YOU WANT TO ARREST SOMEBODY, YOU ARREST THAT FUCKING PSYCHO DOCTOR OVER AT THE HOSPITAL! She didn't even look like herself last time I saw her. She told me herself, there's something off about that bald-headed fuck!"

With that she turned around and stomped off and was gone.

They got back in the car and sat there for a few minutes in the driveway, thinking about what to do next. Rebecca watched them from her front window, her silhouette visible in the glass.

"See anything interesting out back?"

"Just a jungle gym and a sandbox. She's got a kid, I'm assuming. Did she tell you anything?"

"Only that she hates cops as much as Gertrude apparently hates kids. And that there's something off about her doctor - at least according to her."

"She could be covering for her friend. For all we know she's in there with her."

"True. We need to get a search warrant. And we're not leaving until there's somebody outside this house watching it. I want to know if anybody goes in or out."

"I'll make the call. What's next after that? What's our move?"

"There's still one other person who might be able to give us insight into what Gertrude is thinking - where her head is at."

"Who's that?"

"Let's go talk to her doctor."

Escape from the Asylum / Jordan Grupe

6: Bigger Fish to Fry

St. Daniel's Mental Hospital was an enormous and ancient facility. The place spanned an area the size of several city blocks. At the back of the property was a crumbling old manor which was rumored around town to be haunted. The entire hospital was the source of several local legends, the most popular of which pertained to the tunnels beneath it.

It was said there was a labyrinth beneath the hospital - coyly hinted at by the hedge maze that existed aboveground. There were plenty of stories told about the things that happened down there, beneath the sub-basement of the hospital. But those were likely fictitious. Such a place had not even been proven to exist. Still, the stories persisted. Phantoms of patients who attempted to escape the asylum unsuccessfully were said to wander down there. Foolish tales told by teenagers around the campfire, of course. Regardless, it made for interesting modern folklore.

Reynard reached into his pocket and felt for his pills after Dell stepped out of the car. The little blue tablet was easy enough to swallow dry and he did it quickly so his new partner wouldn't notice. The last thing he wanted was for the man to think he was weak somehow.

Every time he came back to this building he got butterflies in his stomach, but this time it was worse than ever. He hated talking to doctors - psychiatrists especially.

His mother had been committed to this very place when he was younger. He had come to visit her on weekends and seen her acting totally unlike herself. She spoke in never-ending sentences, making paranoid statements and ranting about things which made no sense. She was slurring her words and smiling dopily at him the whole time. But his father had insisted on them visiting every week. Towards the end she had acted completely bizarre and unhinged and he had bad memories of those final days with her, ranting and raving and pulling her hair out in clumps.

In the end, she killed herself, although the details of it were still a mystery to him.

Part of him always wondered if what was inside of her mind was also inside of his own, laying dormant and waiting to come out. If one day he would begin to see the spiders crawling on the ceiling, as she had claimed to see. If he would begin to hear the voices whispering in his ear, just as she had.

So far that day had not come - and from what he understood that was a good sign. These illnesses usually presented when people were in their twenties, although it wasn't unheard of for such diagnoses to be made later in life. Still, it meant it had probably skipped a generation. He had loved his mother but he didn't wish her schizophrenia on anyone, and that included himself.

Dell had called ahead to make an appointment with Dr. Mertzek, Gertrude's psychiatrist. He would be in his office waiting for them, according to his secretary.

Entering through the magnetic-lock doors, Reynard hit the button for the elevator. It descended to the ground floor and the doors opened. They stepped inside and immediately noticed there were no buttons. The box was controlled remotely. A security guard spoke to them through an intercom.

"Names please."

"Detective Reynard."

"Detective Dell."

"We're here to see Dr. Mertzek. We have an appointment."

"Hang on. Okay, I see your names here. Just a sec."

The elevator began to move upwards. After a minute it opened and they were greeted by a security guard in a booth, a plexiglass divider separating them.

"ID please, gentlemen."

They pulled out their badges and showed them to the guard.

He inspected them and then passed over a clipboard.

"You'll have to surrender your weapons here. The doctor's office is located in the forensics unit. If you want to go in you'll have to leave your guns outside."

Reynard laughed. The kid looked like he was barely eighteen years old and he wanted possession of his firearm! There was no way that was happening.

"We can't do that. We're on an active murder investigation and they could call us away at any second. How does this usually work? Can your boss come up here and make some sort of exception for us?"

"Uh, yeah I can call him, sure. But I can tell you right now what he'll say. There are no exceptions. You leave the guns or you don't go in."

"Can you ask the doctor to come out here to speak with us, then? I don't like the idea of surrendering my firearm with a fugitive on the loose."

"I'll call him and ask. He doesn't usually leave the unit until it's time to go home, though. It gets pretty busy."

"Try."

The kid went to a phone nearby and picked it up, dialling an extension. He spoke to someone for a minute but Reynard couldn't hear the words. He wrote something down on a piece of paper and hung up a few moments later. Then he came back and shook his head.

"Nope. He's tied up right now with a new admission. Not a good time. But he said to give you this."

He passed him a piece of paper and Reynard read what looked to be an address in the north end.

"What's this?"

"His house. He said to stop by around six tonight and he'll tell you everything he can. The unit is a mess right now, though. We just had a code white and something's got the patients all riled up. He says it's best if you talk later tonight instead."

"Okay. We can do that."

They walked away from the desk, towards the elevator to leave.

"You can do that," said Dell. "We were gonna go back to Rachel's house with the warrant, remember?"

"That's assuming we get it. But yeah, you're right. We probably will. The lieutenant will push hard for it."

"Well, you go to see the doc, I'll go with the team to her place. How's that sound?"

He took the paper from the guard and slipped it into his pocket.

"Sounds like a plan," Reynard said.

It was one decision he would deeply regret in the days to come, but there was no way of knowing that at the time.

The two men got back into the steel box and the doors clanged shut behind them, sealing them inside once again. The same elevator that brought felons recently declared to be insane up to the forensics ward brought them back down to the main level and the doors opened up once again, letting them out.

Reynard's first thought as he stepped outside was that it felt good to be able to breathe again. The air in that place was stuffy and made him feel sick. He didn't want to go back inside ever again - every part of him wanted to avoid the place for the remainder of his days.

But regardless, he had a strong suspicion he would be returning there much sooner than he'd prefer.

7: The Elephant in The Room

Doctor Mertzek had a stunning house. Reynard couldn't help but stare up at it in awe as he pulled up to the place. It was a giant colonial with a well-manicured front lawn surrounded by tall spruce hedges.

A rose garden which featured several different varieties of the flowers flanked the brick walkway leading from the driveway. There, an assortment of luxury automobiles were parked. One of them a black BMW, Reynard couldn't help but notice.

He rang the doorbell and a tall bespectacled man with a white mustache and a bald head answered. His suit was a charcoal grey colour and in his hand was a glass of something brown which Reynard suspected was scotch. He salivated a bit at the mere sight of that brown liquid. An old drinking habit he had mostly gotten over still nagged him from time to time - and after the day he'd just had it was nagging him worse than ever at that moment.

"Detective Franklin Reynard," he said, showing his badge. "Doctor Mertzek, I presume?"

"Yes, pleasure to meet you, although not under these circumstances, of course. Thank you for coming by so late. I hope this wasn't a disruption to your schedule at all?"

"No trouble at all," Reynard said peaceably. "Thank you for having me."

He took his coat and led Reynard into the house. Then the doctor gestured for him to sit down on a supple black leather couch. As he sank into it, he realized it was the most comfortable thing he had ever had the pleasure of resting his oversized ass upon. It was, as the old saying went, soft as a baby's bottom. He reached a hand down to touch it and couldn't understand how anything could possibly be so comfortable.

"Italian leather. It's marvelous, isn't it?" Mertzek asked, standing by the bar. He didn't even need to look at Reynard's expression, the detective thought at first, but then caught the old doctor's reflection in the window glass as he stood there pouring a drink. He was watching him with sly eyes through the mirrored window pane.

"Yes, I have to say... It really is."

Mertzek poured him a glass of something, which was a toasted amber colour. Reynard was about to wave it away, but before he could it was thrust into his upraised hand. Not wanting to show weakness for some reason yet again he found himself accepting it, despite his sobriety.

Upon sniffing and inspecting it did indeed prove itself to be single malt scotch. An older variety which was quite tasty after a sip or two of getting acquainted. Reynard then caught himself taking a very long sip of it despite himself and smacking his lips with pleasure. He told himself to put it on the table and ignore it but was not quite able to.

"You have very fine taste in furniture, doctor. As well as liquor. What is that? Glenfiddich Eighteen year?"

"It's a Macallan eighteen, actually. Although I'm also partial to Glenfiddich. I can get you a glass of that instead, if you prefer?"

Glenfiddich eighteen year sold for about $80 per bottle - Macallan was more than double that.

"No, no. This is perfect. Just what I needed, actually," he said, and realized it was true. "It's been a long day."

He felt himself relaxing despite himself, feeling as if he were sinking deeper and deeper into the cushions of the couch as he sat there, looking at the old doctor's face. It was a *remarkably* comfortable couch.

"Soothing elixir," the doctor said thoughtfully. "I find the Glenfiddich a bit fruitier, while the Macallan simply reeks of sherry. And that subtle hint of toasted oak - perfection!"

He kissed his fingers like a chef to emphasize this. Then he stood and went into the kitchen, excusing himself momentarily.

When he came back into the room he had a charcuterie board balanced upon his fingers like a well-trained waiter. He set it down upon the table in front of Reynard and picked up a piece of what looked to be ham, devouring it while standing.

"I find I never have time to cook for myself these days, with all the responsibilities of the forensics program now weighing upon my shoulders. Once upon a time there were more doctors, more research - but alas, budget cuts."

He motioned to the cutting board covered in cured meats, cheeses, and pickled things.

"Please, help yourself. I have a housekeeper during the day and she does a bit of cooking for me - but since I knew I was having a guest this evening I asked her to make this up for us. Hell on the arteries, of course, but you only live once."

Reynard realized his stomach was rumbling again. It had been almost twelve hours since his half-discarded breakfast at the fast food restaurant.

"Maybe just a few bites," he said, picking up a piece of hard salami and wolfing it down. He swallowed another sip of the Macallan afterwards, revelling in it. It was by far the best scotch he had ever drunk.

"So, Detective. I'm sure you'd like to know about Gertrude Remier. She is the woman of the hour, after all."

"Yes, I have a few questions," Reynard said, although he had momentarily forgotten why he was there amidst the doctor's excellent hospitality. The scotch was lingering on his tongue like the kiss of an old lover after a long absence.

He pulled out his notepad and glanced through it, his eyes suddenly drifting over the pages as if his mind were lost at sea. Suddenly he felt dizzy reading the words he had written down, seasick.

Reynard set down his glass of scotch, feeling ill.

"Are you alright, Detective? You don't look very well."

"I'm good," he lied. "Excuse me, do you have a washroom I could use for a moment?"

"Of course," the doctor said, standing up. "Just this way."

He led Reynard to a bathroom down the hall and he went inside. The room was spinning and he closed the door behind him and locked it, things running through his mind. Thoughts of poisoning and thoughts of murderous doctors, but then another, more sensible idea beneath all of that which he recognized was probably the truth.

He thought back to a half year ago, sitting in his GP's office and discussing his drinking. The words of the old grey-haired man rang in his ear.

"You need to stop. If you don't you're going to kill yourself. Some people get to this stage - like you are now - where you take one drink and you black out. There's no coming back from it when you do damage like that. You need to stop now while you still can."

And he had. But now he was in Dr. Mertzek's house drinking a fine single malt scotch and acting like it was the most normal thing in the world. What had he been thinking?

He splashed cold water on his face and stared at his reflection in the mirror. The eyes which looked back at him were no longer familiar. Red-rimmed and slightly yellow-tinged, a result of his bad habits over the years. The jaundice wouldn't get worse if he stayed off the sauce, but he was no longer off the sauce, was he? He had just given up six months of sobriety on a whim, not wanting to be a bad guest when he wasn't even a guest in this place. He was a homicide detective with a job to do.

His mind was spinning, his thoughts becoming tangential and rambling.

He had given up six months of sobriety...

Not that he went to meetings or had a tangible token like an AA chip for it, but he imagined such a chip in his hand and visualized flushing it down the toilet. Watching it disappear down the pipes.

There was a loud knock at the door and Reynard realized his face felt very cold and slightly uncomfortable on the left side. His eyes were closed and when he opened them he found he was viewing the world from a different angle - one which might be more familiar to a cat. He was down low on the ground, on the floor, looking at the base of the toilet bowl. His cheek was smooshed against the tile floor of the bathroom where piss would spill and dribble from a careless man using the toilet. Not a very sanitary place - but he hadn't been the one to decide to sleep there. His body had made that unconscious decision for him.

"Oh, fuck. Reynard! Are you okay, man!?"

He looked up to see the face of his dead partner staring at him. His eye sockets were empty and leaking dark blood that looked almost black. Those dark empty holes in his head stared at Reynard and bore into him. *Find my killer,* those eyes said.

Blinking, he looked at the face again and realized it was not his old partner's face but his new partner staring at him.

Dell was yelling at him to wake up, looking angry and disgusted with him. The room was still spinning but he managed to pull himself up to sit on the floor.

"I've seen this sort of thing before," the doctor was saying to Dell from the doorway. "I didn't want to get him into trouble, that's why I asked for you specifically. I think he may have a bit of a drinking problem. Drained the entire glass in a minute. Heavens, if I'd known I never would have offered. Just trying to be a good host, but that was foolish of me."

"Please, don't try and blame yourself for this. This is all on *him.*" Dell looked at him with daggers in his eyes as he said this. "He knows better than to drink while he's on the clock, don't you, Reynard?"

He did indeed know better. But that didn't help his pounding headache or his guilty conscience. Only, he didn't remember drinking the entire glass of scotch, only a few sips. Why would the doctor lie about such a thing?

"I barely touched that scotch," he said feebly, the words sounding petty and childish even to his own ears.

The doctor gave Dell a worried look and shook his head with concern. *Poor soul doesn't even remember what happened thirty minutes ago,* that look said.

"I have an early start tomorrow morning," Mertzek said with a hint of annoyance, glancing at his watch. "Can we perhaps get together at another time for this conversation? I'm afraid I am an early riser and also an old man who usually goes to bed by nine thirty every night at the latest."

Dell dragged Reynard to his feet.

"We'll get in touch with you again tomorrow to set up another time to talk. And I'll make sure my partner here is more professional next time - this is an absolute embarrassment. Again, I can't even begin to apologize enough."

The two men left the house, Reynard supported by Dell who put his arm under Reynard's to help hold the man up. They walked over to Dell's car. The doctor was still watching them from the front porch, making sure they were okay.

"So I guess this is what rock-bottom feels like," Reynard said quietly, mostly to himself. But he had no idea what rock-bottom truly felt like. Not yet, anyway.

8: By The Skin of Your Teeth

The next morning Dell really let him have it. As if he didn't feel bad enough already, he quickly felt a hundred times worse.

Gertrude Remier was not found during the execution of the warrant at Rebecca's house and while they had been searching the place, Dell had received the call from the doctor asking for him to come and pick up Reynard (literally) from the bathroom floor. Dell said it had been extremely difficult to think of an excuse fitting enough to explain him leaving the house they were searching *for his case* to go on an unexplained errand.

He had made an excuse about a potential lead in the case, putting his own career on the line with that not-so-little white lie. Lieutenant Snead would surely be asking how that urgent, time-sensitive lead panned out as he was following the case very closely. His own career would be potentially furthered or fucked depending on how it turned out. The mayor and the chief of police were asking for frequent updates and that spur of the moment lie would surely be the subject of the day.

"What exactly was the lead, *Dell*? Where did you have to go in the middle of a search operation, *Dell*? You know I'm new, I'm on thin ice as a rookie detective, and you make me pull that outta my ass to save you from getting disciplined? I should have just let you take the heat. Why didn't I just let you take the heat?"

"Good morning to you too, *Dell*."

"Fuck yourself."

They drove the rest of the way to their destination together in silence. Reynard could already tell it was going to be a long day. Before going to the station for roll call and the daily briefing, they had to stop at the doctor's place again to pick up Reynard's car. He had left it in Mertzek's driveway the night before, since he had been in no state to drive at the time.

Dell pulled up at the curb outside the big house and gave Reynard one last tongue-lashing.

"You know as well as I do we've got limited time to make our case here. Evidence is out there drying up by the minute and we don't have a second to spare. I expected more out of you, Reynard. As somebody who looked up to you for all of five minutes yesterday and thought maybe you were a helluva detective, I hope to hell you can prove to me that's still the case."

"Listen closely, asshole. I appreciate you helping me out last night - just like I would have done for you or any other cop. But let's get one thing straight. I don't owe you shit. I made a mistake and I regret it. I had a few sips of a drink. Now let's move past it and solve this case, alright?"

Dell didn't say anything, he just scowled and waited for Reynard to close his door so he could drive away. He did, then stalked up the driveway and towards his car. The old Crown Victoria looked out of place among the luxury cars parked there. The black BMW was gone now, he noticed.

He got in the car and started it up, was about to drive away, when he saw the housekeeper running out from Mertzek's place. She was wearing an apron and a grey frock, carrying his coat in her hand and waving at him.

"Mister Reynard, Mister Reynard! Your coat, sir. Doctor Mertzek said to make sure you get your coat!"

He realized he had forgotten it the night before but was too embarrassed to say anything to Dell. He had just opted to wear one of his old raincoats instead.

"Thank you, Miss... Sorry, what is your name?"

"Gloria. You are welcome. I very much hope you can find the Doctor's patient. She would be much better off with him, I'm sure. He is a very excellent doctor! The best."

"I'm sure he is, Gloria. Thank you so much, again. I really should be going. Tell Doctor Mertzek thank you again, from me. And apologies."

"Of course, Mister Reynard. I will."

She went inside and Reynard backed out of the driveway and drove the rest of the way to the station.

When he arrived, the bullpen area was empty and he walked through towards the briefing room. He entered through the only door located at the front of the room and realized he was late. The Lieutenant was up front at a podium going through his morning briefing already.

He found a seat at the back of the room and tried to ignore the glares of some of the other, more punctual officers.

"As I was saying... Gertrude Remier is still at large. She is suspected of two murders and is to be considered armed and extremely dangerous. Do not approach her without backup. She has extensive military and weapons training. The firearm taken from Jim... Excuse me, Detective Paulson, still has not been found, meaning she likely has it in her possession. Roadblocks are still in place at all major entry and exit points from town but it is possible she has made her way out somehow using a rural road of some sort that we didn't account for. We've looked over the maps and there are two or three ways she could have gotten around us.

"Furthermore, if that is the case, she is likely still driving the blue Honda Civic seen here in this photo," a large screen TV showed an image from a picture on the security guard's Facebook page. "And she has with her a child, five years of age, named Greg Paulson. For those of you unfamiliar with the case, Miss Remier is the aunt to Greg Paulson and sister-in-law to Detective Paulson who is one of her suspected victims. He was found deceased from his injuries near this phone booth yesterday. We suspect foul play obviously, and we suspect it occurred at the Paulson residence, shown here."

The slide on the large TV screen had been showing the brutal scene of Jim's body and it flipped to the pictures showing the inside of his house - the kitchen covered in blood.

"We've had a few leads but so far no real traction. The window is getting narrower on this one - I'm looking at you Reynard, and you, Dell. DNA is drying up and disappearing in the wind as we speak. We need to have a case ready to go for when we catch this bitch. I want you two out there today busting heads and gathering whatever information you can. The rest of you know your assignments. For those of you at the hospital, I want every inch of that basement searched to find where she was hiding out. Ask the other patients, the staff, anybody who might have talked to Gertrude. We want to know where she's heading."

"For those of you knocking on doors today, there was a report of a suspicious vehicle - a black BMW sedan - which was reportedly occupied for long hours in the neighbourhood adjacent to Detective Paulson's house. It might be nothing, it might be something - just keep it in mind."

He clapped his hands loudly.

"Alright, let's move it! What are we waiting for? Let's find this woman and put her behind bars, okay?"

There was a murmur of agreement around the room, probably not the war cry Snead was expecting. Reynard wondered if they were afraid. Many of them had likely seen the footage of the brutal attack on the guard. The prospect of having to arrest this extremely dangerous and unstable woman was likely sounding terrifying to them at the moment - especially the newer constables and patrolmen.

He shuddered as he thought back to how she had bit off the guard's ear and calmly stuffed it into her front shirt pocket, as if saving it for later.

"Reynard, Dell, in my office," Lieutenant Snead said as people began to file out of the room.

"So, what was this lead yesterday that was so important you had to leave Rebecca Hamstead's house? That *was* your warrant, wasn't it?"

"It's my fault," interjected Reynard. "I was interviewing Gertrude's doctor and I missed his call to go back over there to assist with the search."

"I didn't ask you, Reynard. What the hell was this lead you had to leave right then and there for, Dell? The officers said they barely knew what they were looking for. This could blow the damn case if she was hiding something there."

"I got a call from my C.I.," Dell said, impressing Reynard with the smoothly-told lie. "He said it was something big, and that it couldn't wait. But then he flaked on me. I'll get back in touch with him today."

"You left a search warrant squad in the lurch to go talk to an unreliable rat, is that what you're telling me?" He looked disappointed, on the verge of blowing up, but he didn't. "What else have we got, Reynard? Did the doctor have anything useful to say?"

"Not really," Reynard said. "We're continuing our interview today. He was only available for a short time last night. I'll let you know if I find out anything useful."

"Why the fuck are you two playing games with me? I can expect it from the new guy to some extent, but you, Reynard? Really? Do you get any goddamn leads from him or not?"

Snead wanted something solid. The man looked desperate with his call from the mayor coming in any minute and no new information being provided.

Reynard struggled desperately to think of something the doctor said - anything, that might help. But he came up empty. All they had talked about to his memory was scotch, soft leather, and salami plates. "I got nothing."

Escape from the Asylum / Jordan Grupe

Snead's face went red and a good five minutes of yelling and screaming ensued. They left his office both more than a little bit shaken up. It was becoming obvious that they were highly replaceable at this point - and that their replacements would be taking their spots sooner rather than later if they failed to find any sort of lead soon.

"Sorry," Reynard said to Dell once they were safely out of earshot. "You can put all the blame on me if this goes to hell."

"Oh, you better believe I will. Now come on, you're getting in my car this time. I'll drive today. I don't trust you behind the wheel after last night."

That comment drew a few glances from people in the bullpen and he shot Dell a look that told him he didn't appreciate it. Dell ignored it completely. "We're going back to the hospital. I'm gonna take the lead today."

Reynard followed after him, grunting his permission. In reality, he had lost all control of the investigation. Even he knew that. The Lieutenant might have been more approving of his actions so far over Dell's, but he didn't know the truth. And if he did he'd be furious. It could be the end of his career.

He had no choice but to follow his young, inexperienced partner's lead. When the other man's back was turned he grabbed the pill bottle from his pocket and shook one of the little pills loose into his hand, dry-swallowing it. His racing thoughts were bad but the headache he had was far worse - not alleviated by sleep, it was brewing like a dark cloud between his temples. A thunderhead which sent bolts of pain to his eyes which felt full of pressure. Every time he looked at a light he couldn't help but wince.

He tried to shake off these feelings and focus on the problem at hand. There was a missing five year old boy out there and a psychopathic murderer was currently holding him hostage. She had killed his partner and another innocent man only a day before. It was time to focus. To find her. All he could do was hope that it was not already too late.

9: A Perfect Storm

By the time they reached the hospital Reynard's headache had only gotten worse. Every pair of headlights which drove past on the rain-slicked road blinded him and made his eyes and his head throb with pressure-pain. When they pulled into the parking spot out front, Dell looked at him in concern.

"Are you okay? You look a bit pale, Reynard."

"I'll be fine. I just need a coffee. Maybe they've got a cafe inside."

"We're here to investigate a murder, man. Not to eat breakfast."

"Fuck, I can't win with you, can I?"

They left it at that and walked into the building without talking. The rain had been pouring off and on for three days now and there was no sign of it letting up. The weather man on the radio said it would be like that for at least another week, if not more.

Once they got inside they proceeded through the small entryway and into the main corridor. To the left of where they stood, the crime scene was still blocked off with yellow caution tape. The blood had been cleaned up now but it was still a point of interest that they didn't want disturbed any more than necessary. After another 24 hours or so they would have to relinquish control of that section of the hospital once again, though. A uniformed officer stood sentry just inside the double glass doors and he nodded at them curtly.

A security guard flagged them down and came over to them. It was the same short, brown haired guard who had shown them the security camera footage the day prior.

"Hey, you're back," he said. "I've got something for you. I was gonna give you a call actually. Turns out one of the patients I talked to says she knew Gertrude. Used to go outside with her for a cigarette every now and then. I convinced her you were cool, and eventually she said she'd talk to you. She isn't the most talkative, but she feels bad about the whole thing. That guard was kind of an asshole, truth be told, but he didn't deserve that."

"Nobody deserves that," Reynard said, motioning to the room adjacent to them which had been painted with blood the day prior.

Dell, who had not yet seen the tape but had read the report, looked unconcerned.

"Where's this patient? Can you set up a private place for us to talk with her?"

"Yeah, you can use the room next to the security office. It's empty. I'll see if I can find her out front smoking - that's where she usually is."

"Thanks," Reynard said. "We appreciate your help. What's your name, by the way?"

"Matthew. And it's no problem. Anything I can do, really."

They sat waiting in the small office for Matthew to come back with the patient. It didn't take long.

The woman sat down across from them at the small wooden table and didn't make eye contact. She fidgeted and crossed her legs, shifting her gaze from the clock to the door to the table to her feet then back again. Her shirt displayed a screaming skull face which was on fire and the name (presumably) of a death metal band.

"Hi. My name is Detective Reynard. This is Detective Dell. We were hoping to find out some information about a patient here - Gertrude Remier. Do you know her very well?"

"Not that well," the woman said after a long pause. "We were pretty close for a while there. But not so close that she told me what she planned to do."

"What did she tell you?"

"That she didn't belong here. She said it was all a big misunderstanding - whatever it was that got her put in this place. She never did tell me the specifics of it. But she said that if she got out she wouldn't try to get revenge, she'd just try to get away from here."

Reynard made a note of this in his book while Dell simply listened.

"Did she ever talk about meeting up with anyone on the outside? When she finally did get out?"

The woman thought about this for a minute.

"Y'know, it's funny... Back at the start, she'd talk about 'them' and how she couldn't wait to see 'them' when she was finally free - again no specifics on who 'they' were. But then after a while she just said she couldn't wait to see 'him.' Singular. Whoever else she'd been looking forward to seeing after getting out, they didn't seem to matter anymore. Made me wonder if she had a boyfriend who dropped her when he found out where she was."

An idea was beginning to form in Reynard's mind. A theory that he found utterly disturbing, but that made it no less plausible.

"We're trying to figure out where she would have gone. Do you have any idea what sort of destination she might have in mind? Did she ever say anything to you about where she wanted to go after she got out of here?"

Her eyes looked far off and strange for a minute, then she said something unexpected.

"Not specifically. She said she liked to get out of the city in the summer, though. That she had a place up north."

The two detectives looked at each other and nodded meaningfully. The family cottage up north was looking like a more likely hideout every minute.

Escape from the Asylum / Jordan Grupe

"You guys will tell the team that I cooperated with you, right? It might help me get out of here sooner if they... Can you? Please?"

"Of course," Dell said. "We'd be happy to."

She excused herself and left quietly, leaving the two detectives alone again.

"What do you think?" asked Dell.

"I think we need to check out that cottage, ASAP."

"It's a five hour drive from here. How are we gonna do that, exactly? We've got a million things to do around here. How do we even know she's telling the truth?"

"Either way, it's worth checking out. Why don't you call the Lieutenant and mention it to him? Maybe it'll put you back in his good graces if we have a lead to follow up on."

Dell looked at him with a side-eye that made Reynard feel certain he was still mad about the night prior. He definitely didn't trust him. Still, his new partner left the small side room office and Reynard was alone with his thoughts for a minute - just as he had wanted.

His mind suddenly felt like it was swimming again, like he was underwater and gasping for air, the same as the night before with the doctor. What was causing the sensation, he wasn't sure.

Suddenly his phone rang with an unexpected call. He answered it with shaking hands, trying to calm himself enough to speak to whoever was on the other end. It felt important that he did.

10: Down The Rabbit Hole

"Detective Reynard, is that you?" The woman on the other end of the line sounded frightened, on the verge of panic.

"Yes, who is this?"

"This is Allison Paulson. Are you alone?"

"I am. Why? Are you okay? You're still at the hotel, right? Did something happen?"

"Don't ask questions, there isn't time. I *need you to know. You have to stop her. You're the only one who can.*"

"Allison, I'm doing everything in my power, trust me."

The sound of a child crying could be heard in the background. It was a young boy. "I want my mommy!" he was yelling. "Auntie Gertrude, please! I want my mommy!"

"Shhhh! Mommy is talking on the phone!"

That was when it hit him - this wasn't Allison calling from the hotel. It was Gertrude pretending to be Allison. He opened the office door and waved Dell back in, indicating silently for him to tell the Lieutenant to track the call. "It's you... Gertrude, wherever you are, just turn yourself in. We're going to find you sooner or later. Let the boy go home to his mother. He's scared, I can hear him crying. He wants to go home, he said it himself!"

"HE DOESN'T KNOW WHAT HE WANTS! Don't you get it?" she hissed. "She isn't me! This isn't her! She carved my face! She did! Nobody listens to me! Nobody ever listens!" She sounded completely mad, but he knew enough of interrogations not to dispute her claims. It was better to indulge her.

"Alright, Allison, then. Why don't you come back and talk to us. Explain what happened and we'll fix things." Reynard's head was spinning. He was having trouble focusing, his head splitting with an early morning migraine.

She sighed on the other end of the phone, sounding exasperated. "You don't believe me... Nobody ever fucking believes me!"

The line went dead in his hand and he stared at it dumbly, wondering what he said wrong. Then he realized it wasn't what he'd said, but how he'd said it. "She hung up," he said to Dell. "Did they get a trace?"

His partner was talking rapidly on the phone but his voice sounded far-off and strange suddenly, as if being heard from the other end of a long tunnel. That was when the room began to spin round and round in circles. He looked over at Dell's face and saw it was morphing, changing into something different. The young stern-faced man was laughing at him, his eyes rolling back in his head and new ones bulging from his bloated cheeks that looked like they belonged to an insect of some sort.

The shadows in the room started looming larger over him, the one behind the coat rack looking like a menacing phantom. The paint on the walls was melting like candle wax, he noticed with alarm. "Is it a fire? Is that why you're melting," he asked, knowing that sounded wrong. "What's wrong with your eyes, Dell? There's something wrong with your eyes..."

The thoughts were racing through his mind and he felt he couldn't control the spiralling feeling taking him downwards into an abyss in his mind. Something else popped into his head and before he could stop himself he was saying it out loud - although he wouldn't remember it until much later. "The doctor! Don't let that doctor near me! He killed my mother!" After those words he slumped over and fell to the floor. Dell almost caught him, but not quite, and he sustained a hard knock to his head on the way down. While he lay on the floor he saw the room was spinning in circles all around him and he heard a voice shouting for help, shouting loudly for someone to call an ambulance. "There's a lot of blood," the voice was saying. "Tell them to hurry!"

11: Adding Insult to Injury

Reynard woke up feeling fuzzy and wrong. His mind was swimming and he was having trouble focusing. Looking around, he saw he was in an unfamiliar bed in an unfamiliar room.

A woman dressed in regular street clothes entered and walked over to him with a concerned look on her face.

"You're awake," she said. "How are you feeling?"

"Who are you?" Just speaking out loud seemed to hurt. A piercing needle of pain seemed to dig in through his eye and into his brain.

"Ugh... My head..."

"You had a bad fall. Ended up with a cut on your forehead. But it was patched up easy enough. How are you feeling?" she repeated the question as if he hadn't heard her.

"Sore. Where's my coat? Shit, where are my pants for Chrissake!?"

He looked down to see he was now clothed in a hospital gown. His pants, wallet, coat, even his gun, they were all missing. He felt a moment of embarrassment realizing this stranger could see his junk.

"Where are my things?" He asked, anger beginning to boil up within him. "What the hell happened to my..."

He tried to stand up and slumped right back down onto the bed. It felt as if he could pass out again at any moment.

"You had an episode. In the office downstairs. Dr. Mertzek told us to bring you up here and have you lie down for a little while. He wanted to be notified as soon as you woke up."

That name sent alarm bells ringing in his mind. But when he tried to decide why he could not. His recent memory was a shifting black void, only bits and pieces of it recognizable.

"Doctor... No, I don't need to see any doctor. I'm fine. How long was I out?"

She slipped out of the room quickly without answering and muttered something about being right back. He recognized the look of concern on her face and realized he had said something wrong.

"Hey!"

He shouted after her, but she didn't return.

Nearly an hour later, his thoughts finally swimming round his mind again like familiar goldfish, she finally came back with an apologetic look on her face.

"I'm so sorry, Mr. Reynard! Something happened and I couldn't get back right away. Are you doing alright?"

"No, I'm not alright! Where is Doctor Mertzek!? I demand to be released immediately! I'm being held here against my will and I..."

The door swung open and the doctor came in behind her. He looked down disapprovingly from his high vantage point. The man had to be over six and a half feet tall, easily.

"Hello, Detective Reynard. I'm glad to see you're awake. My apologies for the delay. What seems to be the problem?"

"The problem? You locked me in here and you're keeping me against my will! That's my problem."

Dr. Mertzek smiled faintly.

Escape from the Asylum / Jordan Grupe

"I can assure you, Detective, we would never do that to you. This door has been unlocked the whole time. Did you ever attempt to open it?"

Reynard had no idea what to say. His face was suddenly hot and red with embarrassment. He stood up, or tried to, and once again fell back down onto the bed. The room was spinning badly all around him.

"Are you certain you're alright, Detective? Here, stand up and walk with me. I'll drive you home myself."

He held out his hand for Reynard to take.

"Well, are you coming?" The doctor asked, the same insufferable smile etched on his face.

"My legs, they're feeling very weak all of a sudden. And the room.... It won't stop spinning... Where's my partner?"

"Your partner left quite some time ago, Detective. He left you in our care."

"He did what!? Where's my phone? I need to speak to him."

Reynard's memories still resolving in his mind, he suddenly remembered that he did not trust this man. Not even a little bit.

Mertzek put up a finger as if to say, "Just a minute," and left, coming back with Reynard's phone in his hand.

"Here you are. Your cell phone as requested. I'll give you some privacy. When you're ready to leave just put on the call bell and the nurses will help you up in a wheelchair."

Reynard began to scroll through his contacts and realized he didn't have Dell's number in his phone yet.

"Ah, yes, sorry I nearly forgot. Your partner left me his number. Here," Mertzek passed him a small scrap of paper with a phone number on it. "By the way, Detective, I highly recommend you go speak to your doctor immediately. I've spoken to your

Lieutenant already and told him he should give you the day off to rest."

The news just got better and better, didn't it? He didn't want time off. That was the last thing he wanted at that moment.

What he needed was his coat. He needed that very badly but didn't see it anywhere in the room. That fact did not surprise him considering his newfound suspicions regarding the doctor.

He forced himself to smile politely.

"Alright. Thank you Doctor Mertzek," Reynard said with as much forced politeness as he could muster. "If you could ask the nurses to grab that wheelchair sooner rather than later, I'd appreciate it. And my coat, please."

"Of course. I'll ask them to get it now for you."

He managed to mumble another terse, "Thank you," before dialling Dell's number into his phone.

It rang a few times and Reynard had a horrible feeling that he wouldn't pick up or that Mertzek had given him the wrong number - intentionally or otherwise - but then Dell answered.

"Detective Dell speaking," he said.

"Dell, it's Reynard! What the hell happened? You gotta come get me, I'm at the mental hospital. There's something really weird going on," he said, then stopped himself, realizing someone could be at the door listening.

"Reynard. You okay? You took a pretty bad spill there… And you were talking about all kinds of really fucked up shit. Mertzek thought maybe you were having a mental break."

"You can't believe anything he says," Reynard whispered harshly. "I can't talk now, but I'll explain later."

Dell let out an exasperated sigh.

"Can I be honest, Reynard? I don't trust *you* right now. Not that this was your fault today but you have been the *most unreliable partner I've ever seen.* I'm sorry. I know you're my senior and everything but this is getting ridiculous. This is the biggest case this town has seen - well, ever - and you're just... I don't know what you're doing."

"*I'm working the case, Dell. Okay?*"

"Okay, listen, I gotta go. I'm following up on a lead. I've got Burns with me and Lieutenant Snead wants you home for the rest of the day to recuperate. Just try to get your head straight and stay out of the fucking liquor cabinet, alright? Oh, and you can thank me later for not telling anybody the crazy shit you were saying before you went out."

Reynard found himself wishing he hadn't given Dell such a hard time in the beginning.

"I owe you one hell of an apology, Dell. For being such an asshole. But trust me, I'm a good detective. And I'll prove it to you. I'll call you as soon as I'm feeling up to moving around."

"...Alright," Dell said hesitantly.

"Ready to go?" Doctor Mertzek asked, barging into the room. "Oh, I'm sorry. I hope I'm not interrupting. I can come back."

"No, no, please. I'm done. Thanks, Dell. Think about what I said, okay? I'll talk to you soon."

He looked up at Dr. Mertzek and an older nurse who was standing next to him, snapping rubber gloves onto her hands.

"All set?" the doctor asked. "Your chariot awaits."

He nodded and they helped him up into a wheelchair, which he nearly collapsed into. Mertzek pushed Reynard out of the room and up the hall. "I've got it from here, Alice. I'll take him down to where he needs to be."

Escape from the Asylum / Jordan Grupe

12: Live and Learn

Dr. Mertzek pushed Reynard along in the wheelchair, the old bearings squeaking as it went down the hallways. He exited the unit and Reynard looked down at his wrist and was surprised to see a patient armband there.

"What's this," he asked, inspecting it.

"Ah, yes. For the medication - we had to register you in order to prescribe it through our system."

"Medication? What medication?"

Mertzek cleared his throat. He spoke, sounding uncomfortable.

"I'd prefer not to speak of it in the hallway like this, Detective. It isn't appropriate. Patient confidentiality - I could be sued."

"Sued for what? Just tell me what the hell you gave me!"

He was raising his voice but no longer cared.

"An injectable medication called Lorazepam, Detective. It assists in stopping seizures lasting more than a few minutes. Most Grand Mal Seizures - as they are colloquially called - last for less than a couple minutes. But the really bad ones, the really dangerous ones, go on and on and on, and they just never end. Isn't that horrible, Detective Reynard?"

"Yes, horrible."

"So we injected you with a bit of that medication in order to assist with that particular... problem that you were having. Now, can we lay this to rest for the time being? I think it's important that you focus on your recovery. Oh, and by the way, no driving at all for now. Can you imagine if you had an event like that on the road, behind the wheel? Well, you could kill a lot of people, Reynard. It's best for you to remain in the passenger seat for now. That's doctor's orders."

Escape from the Asylum / Jordan Grupe

Reynard's blood was boiling. He suddenly felt so fragile, so old, so vulnerable and weak as this older man pushed him down the hallway in a wheelchair - while he was unable to hold himself upright.

Mertzek pushed him into an elevator and turned him around to face the door. Then he hovered his hand over the buttons for a moment, looking like he was trying to decide. Someone else got into the elevator and he quickly hit the button for the lobby.

"Can we stop by the police station before you take me home? I want to see somebody there real quick," he managed to say, his words coming with difficulty.

"I have a very busy day ahead of me, Detective, is that really necessary?"

"I'm afraid it is. Evidence. It can't wait. This would delay the investigation. You wouldn't want that, would you, doctor?"

He took the silence as a small victory and eventually the old man relented and said he would stop by the police station as requested.

The roads were clogged with traffic and Mertzek complained the whole way, saying that he didn't have time for such things, but Reynard made no concessions. And by the time they got to the police station, he was beginning to feel somewhat clear again.

He got out of the car and stood up on his own two feet.

"I'll take it from here, doctor. I feel much better, thank you."

"Really, Detective, I don't think that's a good-" he shouted after him, but Reynard was already inside. He smirked, feeling satisfied, as the doors closed behind him while Mertzek was mid-sentence.

"Self righteous, pompous piece of... " he was muttering to himself when his boss happened to walk past.

"Reynard! Good to see you up and about. I heard you were out of commission for at least the rest of the day today. What the hell is going on with you lately?"

"I'm sorry, Lieutenant. I'll go see my GP. It was probably just low blood sugar or something."

"That's not what the doctor's telling us from over there. What's his name? Mertz-something?"

"Mertzek. What's he saying about me?"

"Not much yet, I'm supposed to meet with him today. He just told me you had a seizure. You coulda been toast if you hadn't been at the hospital, that's what he told me. Not to mention the fact that you aren't supposed to drive anymore. Hell if I know how we're gonna swing that. Dell will have to be your designated driver until we can get it sorted out. Speaking of which, how'd you get back here? I thought your shithead partner was out on a lead."

"I got an Uber, and give Dell a break, Snead - not his fault the C.I. flaked on him. You know they're not the most reliable bunch."

That was what Reynard thought he had said out loud, but then realized he had only said it in his own mind. He was suddenly unable to talk. His voice box was paralyzed and he could only stare at the Lieutenant as he gaped at him.

He realized there were people all around him, standing in the foyer, staring at him as he tried futilely to say something. The lights in the room were glowing too bright.

"I need to go to my office," he managed in a choked whisper, feeling increasingly ill. The walls felt like they were closing in around him. His clothes felt too hot and too tight around his neck.

He stumbled away from the Lieutenant and got on the elevator. He stuck his thumb up and tried to smile as the doors closed. Quickly hitting the button for the homicide floor, he leaned on the wall and took a few deep breaths. "You're fine. Just breathe."

Escape from the Asylum / Jordan Grupe

Suddenly he had a thought. He hit the button for a different floor instead. The laboratory.

"I need these analyzed. It's for the Gertrude Remier case," he mumbled to the lab technician. "Get it done as fast as you can."

"You need to fill out a requisition," he told Reynard with a concerned look. "You can't just leave these here without filling out the paperwork first. Chain of possession, you know that. Hey, are you alright? You don't look so good."

Resignedly, Reynard took the paperwork back to his office with the pills to try and fill them out. The room was spinning again and it was getting harder and harder to keep his eyes open. Who the hell knew what the doctor had been feeding him at the hospital - but he doubted it was Lorazapam. That was the same thing he took for anxiety and he had never felt like that before.

Now that he thought about it, he should get his blood checked too. He decided he'd photocopy one of the forms and give them a vial of blood while he was at it. But he'd have to go to an outside lab for the bloodwork draw - it was far too complicated to do it at the station. It would be impossible to explain - this was all guesswork and utter conjecture at this point.

If Snead found out he was investigating the doctor instead of Gertrude, he'd be in deep shit. But he knew the man was involved somehow. And besides, there were uniformed officers out on the hunt for Gertrude. They were looking for her everywhere. He needed to figure out what was happening underneath it all. And the doctor was part of that. Somehow, he was sure of it.

He managed to get back to his office after making his photocopies, looking completely drunk while he did so and getting stares from the entire office.

Slumped over at his desk, he fell asleep trying to fill out the forms.

His dreams were long and terrible.

13: Don't Get Bent Out of Shape

Reynard was in the wheelchair again, being pushed along by Doctor Mertzek. At least he assumed it was him, there was no real way of knowing who was behind him, propelling him down the fluorescent-lit corridor.

Down the polished, gleaming hallways they went, through the pale yellow-walled corridors of the mental hospital. And then they got to the elevator. It yawned wide before them like a giant mouth, the doors opening up and down, rather than to the sides. Surreal and terrifying in a way that only dreams can manage.

The man behind him spun him around and backed him in, then stood beside him in the elevator. Reynard suddenly realized he had a straightjacket on. And the man standing next to him was indeed the doctor who he feared so badly now. The old man reminded him of all the doctors who had looked down at him when he'd asked about his mother's condition all those years ago, who had disdained him and made him feel so small and stupid.

Mertzek pushed the button to go down and smiled at Reynard. "We'll get you all fixed up," he said, as if he *were* a child. "You won't have to worry about a thing anymore! We're going to take care of everything for you now."

What was that supposed to mean? He wanted to ask but found he couldn't speak aloud. There was a ball-gag in his mouth.

Reynard realized the button illuminated on the elevator panel was "B2" - the sub basement. *Why are we going to the sub basement?* He wanted to ask, but couldn't. He couldn't say or do anything. He was paralyzed in the straightjacket, his legs tied down tightly, his mouth gagged so he couldn't speak. His hands felt numb as if the restraints were too tight, cutting off the circulation.

"I've got something very important to show you downstairs, Reynard. Just you wait," he whispered in his ear, making the hairs stand up on the back of his neck.

The doors to the elevator opened and Reynard saw there was only blackness beyond the box they were in. Mertzek pushed him out into this darkness, whistling a happy tune. As he strode away from the elevator, the doors shut behind them and he was left in the blackness with the mad doctor as he whistled and pushed him forward, into the void.

They went along these completely blackened hallways and the doctor continued whistling, but then the sound of it began to recede into the background. He was still being propelled forward somehow, but the doctor was no longer pushing him as the wheelchair picked up speed and went faster and faster down the narrow, blackened hallway of the sub basement.

Despite the darkness, Reynard glimpsed faces from the intersecting corridors occasionally, passing by faster and faster as he picked up speed. Twisted, smiling faces with rotten teeth and blackened gums. He saw them lurking in the shadows, watching as he flew past them in his wheelchair, out of control.

And then he saw the door, straight ahead. It was the door of a patient's room from a century and a half ago, back when the hospital had been built. It was a thick studded door with a small barred window at the top, not even big enough for a hand to go through.

He raced towards it and thought he would slam into it full force, bracing for the impact of it. But then the door swung open inwards, revealing an even blacker space inside.

The wheelchair flew in through the open door and then he crashed into a wall on the other side, hitting his forehead hard against the stone. Reynard saw stars spinning round him in circles as he laid there with his forehead against the hard stone floor. Blood was leaking from his nose and it was warm on his face, then quickly became cold in the damp chill of the room. He slept.

14: On Thin Ice

REYNARD! REYNARD! A voice in his mind was shouting. He was still locked in the cell. What was the point of getting up when he was trapped here against his will? He would be better off just giving up, ignoring them. So he did.

REYNARD! WAKE UP! WAKE UP REYNARD!

The voice was insistent. Suddenly there was a sharp pinch above his left eye. It hurt badly.

"REYNARD! WAKE THE FUCK UP!"

His head bolted up from the desk and he realized he had been sleeping. No, not sleeping. He had been knocked out by something. That fucking doctor had drugged him! He knew it was Mertzek somehow.

"What the hell's the matter with you, Reynard?" Snead asked, standing over him. "I just finished talking with Dr. Mertzek and he's convinced you're mentally unfit for duty right now. He said he told you that but you decided to keep it from me? Not only that, but I come in here to find you like this?? What in the actual fuck is wrong with you?"

There was blood all over his hands, Reynard realized suddenly. And all over the desk and the papers he had been filling out. Everything was soaked in his blood and he didn't know where it was coming from at first. Then he realized it seemed to be still leaking from his nose.

"I don't know…" he said feebly. "I think that doctor… I think he slipped me something."

"That's a very serious accusation," Lieutenant Snead said, his hands on his hips. "Do you have any proof of it? Why didn't you tell me this until now?"

"I was so messed up I could barely stand upright. I was trying to prove it before making any accusation, but I couldn't even get through these forms without passing out. I think it's finally made its way out of my system, for the most part - whatever it was. But this damn nosebleed, this shit is new."

Snead handed him a box of tissues from the other side of the desk.

"Thanks."

The old lieutenant seemed to think this new information over carefully. He asked the next question hesitantly, almost apologetically.

"You have a family history of... certain types of... conditions... Do you not, Reynard?"

He had never told Snead about his mother. He felt his face turning red and hot with anger.

"Excuse me, sir?"

"Ahem, pardon me for asking. Normally I wouldn't bring it up but under these circumstances I feel like it's relevant."

"What's relevant?"

"Your mother, Reynard. She was admitted to that same hospital, no? Mertzek said he was a resident back then, that he was part of the team that treated her. She had similar symptoms, according to him."

Of course Mertzek had treated his mother. It made a sick sort of sense. He had probably met the man as a child, that was why he was so terrified of him. At least that was a small part of the reason.

"This is bullshit," Reynard snapped. "That sonofabitch is trying to get away with murder and he's trying to make me look crazy because I'm on to him."

"Murder? Whose murder?"

He thought about it for a minute. No, Mertzek didn't murder anyone, that was true. So why was he investigating him? He had poisoned him, that was why. Or had he? Had it just been his old, feeble body no longer being able to handle liquor anymore, just as his doctor had predicted? Could that have caused the hallucinations, the seizure, the complete collapse he had experienced?

His thoughts were racing a mile a minute and he couldn't figure out what his plan was anymore or who he was against or what he was trying to accomplish. It had started off so simple - they had been trying to catch Gertrude. But what if Gertrude wasn't really Gertrude? What if she was Allison? It sounded ridiculous at first, but now he wasn't so sure.

He would need proof, though. And he still didn't know if he believed it himself.

"Please, trust me, there's something up with that doctor. Just get these tested."

He held up the bloodied bottles containing his extra strength acetaminophen and another which contained prescription pills for anxiety. Little blue tablets in a tinted yellow container with a white cap.

"These are yours?" Snead asked, reading the label.

"They were. I think he tampered with them. I think Mertzek is trying to poison me. That's the only thing that makes any fucking sense, considering what's been happening to me."

"Okay, we'll test them. But in the meantime, you're going to the hospital."

He stopped when he saw Reynard's expression.

"Not St. Daniel's. The medical hospital. They can run some blood tests on you and see what's going on with you and why you're having these hallucinations and seizures. I need your gun and badge until we get it figured out. You can't keep your service weapon if you're hallucinating and having seizures - you just can't. We'll get this straightened out then we'll talk about it again."

Snead said this last statement with no inflection, as if he were asking Reynard for his coffee order. He handed over the badge and gun with a shaking hand, feeling resentful.

"I'll get someone to drive you to the hospital. You're not allowed behind the wheel of a car, not until you get the all-clear from a doctor."

He stayed in the hospital overnight due to lingering symptoms of *epistaxis* as they called it (nose bleeding in layman's terms) and hypotension. His blood pressure was so low it drew a few strange glances from nurses checking it. They ended up transfusing him with several units of blood after the nosebleed wouldn't stop for hours and investigated him for internal bleeding, but they found none.

"Do you have blood taken often?" one of the nurses asked when she was taking another sample.

"Just today," he responded. She was not the first one to stab him with a needle in the hospital that afternoon. Most of the attempts to draw blood had been unsuccessful, as if he had none left inside of him.

"You're a really tough poke. If I don't get it this time I'll see if somebody else can give it a try."

She poked him again with a fresh needle.

"Damn, missed again. Alright, let me see if Leslie's around. She'll get you."

But Leslie couldn't get it either. The doctor had to come in and take it with an exasperated look on his face which said this was not his job. After several minutes he managed to find a vein.

Several different doctors came in after that to speak with him and he lost track of their names and specialities.

Eventually one woman came in with her hair done up in a tight bun. She had thick black-rimmed glasses and bright red painted nails. In her arms she carried a clipboard, but no stethoscope or other medical instruments like the other doctors had carried.

She didn't listen to his heart sounds or order blood work samples to be drawn, she simply spoke with him at length. The topics of discussion made Reynard oddly uncomfortable.

"Have you ever had thoughts of hurting yourself or anyone else," she asked at one point and he finally bristled to the point of confirming his suspicion.

"What sort of doctor are you exactly?" he asked.

"I'm a psychiatrist, Mr. Reynard. Sorry, I should have told you that right away. Your team thought it would be wise to get my opinion."

"Your opinion on what, exactly?"

She shuffled in her chair a bit and looked uncomfortable. Instead of answering, she asked another question.

"I understand it was your assertion that Dr. Mertzek poisoned you somehow? What made you so sure?"

"You wouldn't happen to know Dr. Mertzek personally, would you? Are you a colleague of his?"

She looked at him with an unreadable expression on her face.

"I can assure you, I'm a completely unbiased outlet for you to talk about these things. I have no affiliation with him whatsoever and, to be frank, my opinions of him are neutral at best. So, please, give me your honest recollections. Why did you feel that you had been poisoned, specifically by this doctor?"

"It all started the night of the murders. He invited me to his house to speak about the case and he offered me a drink. It was single malt scotch - a very expensive variety. Macallan eighteen year. I started feeling funny after taking a sip."

Or two or three, he thought but didn't say. *Surely it was no more than that.*

"I see. You're sure it was just a sip? Is it possible you just had a low tolerance for alcohol? I'm just playing devil's advocate here."

He nodded, feeling guilty.

"And, Mr. Reynard, may I ask, have you ever had issues with alcohol in the past? Specifically, has it ever caused you to collapse in a similar fashion?"

He thought about this long and hard. It pained him to admit she was right.

"Yes. A few times. I was advised not to drink again by my doctor. He told me it would be very bad if I kept drinking so I quit. He said it was starting to affect my liver."

"Correct. I see in your medical records that he requested a consultation with an expert who did some tests and it showed elevated levels of certain liver enzymes indicating liver failure. Does that sound familiar?"

"Yes."

"And have you ever heard of hepatic encephalopathy, Detective?"

He sighed. He had done research into what would happen to him later on, once his liver truly began to give out. On those lonely, long nights when the liquor store seemed so close and his mouth seemed so dry.

"Yes, I've researched it a bit."

"So then you realize it could explain some of the symptoms you've been having. The hallucinations, the disorientation, the distrust bordering on paranoia, the balance issues."

"Wait, just tell me... Did you check for toxicology? Was I poisoned or not?"

"No, Mr. Reynard. You were not poisoned. Nothing on the toxicology report indicated any substance was used to intoxicate you aside from your own prescription Lorazepam and the dose of the same medication that the doctor administered to you to stop the seizures at the hospital. Which, by the way, probably saved your life. If he had wanted you dead he could have easily just let you continue without administering anything."

"And the pills? What about the pills I gave to Snead?"

"Just plain old tylenol and Lorazepam. The only thing we could find that was strange was that you had a slightly elevated INR which indicates an issue with clotting - hence your bloody nose. But you can speak with your family doctor about that further. It's likely genetic. We're more concerned with these other developments. We've been running some liver enzyme tests and the results are not particularly encouraging... I would recommend a CAT scan, even an MRI, personally, but I see that the medical team has already ordered those. Can I ask, what were you taking the Lorazepam for?"

"Anxiety. I get anxious sometimes since my wife died," he answered quietly. It had actually started after his mother died, but had gotten worse over the years, becoming overwhelming with the passing of Nadine.

"Ah, fair enough. I can see I've upset you. I think that's enough questions for now. I'll speak to you more after your CT scan, how's that?"

Terrible, he wanted to say. He was supposed to be out catching a serial killer but instead he was trapped inside a hospital emergency room on a lumpy stretcher getting tests. One test after another, his ass getting numb from laying still. But he wasn't allowed to leave. And he wasn't allowed to drive.

He had a strange feeling that was exactly what Doctor Mertzek and Gertrude Remier wanted. And for the first time but not the last, it occurred to him that the two of them could be working together. How that was possible he didn't know, but he intended to find out.

15: A Blessing in Disguise

After spending too many hours in the hospital, Reynard checked himself out against the doctor's advice.

He was sick of all the tests. When he asked what their plan was, they told him they were going to do even more tests, and keep him overnight, since there was such a long wait for the MRI. And they planned to do more blood work. And more X-rays and EEGs. This information was difficult to obtain as the doctors and nurses disappeared for long stretches and were reluctant to tell him anything except to wait and see.

He eventually tore off the hospital armband and walked out. He called a cab, tired of it all. The car pulled up and he got inside, feeling naked somehow without his badge and his gun - but at least a little less naked now that he had pants on. The hospital gowns left little to the imagination.

"Where to?" the driver asked, looking in the mirror.

It was the first he had thought about it. The moon was high in the sky, fat and full, and the air was warm considering the time - just past midnight. He didn't want to go home. He wasn't tired. There was only one place he wanted to go.

The place from his dream. The place where this had all started.

"Take me to St. Daniel's Mental Hospital," he said.

The driver gave him a strange look in the mirror.

"You know visiting hours are over, right?"

"Just take me there. I'm a cop. I've got something to look into."

Escape from the Asylum / Jordan Grupe

The driver didn't say another word, looking nervous after the word *'cop'*. Some cab drivers sold weed and coke on the side, he had seen in his days. Part of him wondered if maybe this guy was slinging something. If he did, he was smooth enough to act natural for the rest of the drive, making casual conversation about the local football team. The truth was, Reynard could care less about a low level weed dealer - people could buy the stuff at the corner store these days, after all.

Regardless, he managed to get him to his destination quickly enough. The traffic was light at this time of the evening and they arrived at the hospital minutes later. He thanked the man and left him a good tip, stepping back out into the night air and breathing in deeply.

Reynard had asked the driver to drop him off at the back of the property, near an old manor that was located back there. It would be good cover for him as he approached the grounds in the darkness. He wasn't sure what he was looking for, but it would be inside, in the sub basement. And he didn't want to look during daylight hours.

He just needed to find a way in.

Sneaking along the roadways leading towards the main building, he stuck to the shadows, trying to avoid the streetlights. Raccoons scurried past at one point, startling him, jumping out of dumpsters when he walked by. Bats were flapping silently through the sky above, chasing bugs in large numbers.

The old manor was supposedly haunted, that was the word around town, anyways. The whole hospital was supposed to be inhabited by ghosts and the spirits of restless souls who had died in the place. But the manor had a special quality about it - a darkness and a malevolence that could not be ignored by the casual passerby. People posted online about the building, taking pictures after breaking into the place. It was illegal obviously, but that didn't stop anyone.

There were several pictures of the place which could be found online (on ghost-hunting websites) showing a face in one of the windows on the second floor in particular. The same window every time, and the same face. A young girl. She looked out with a sad expression, almost transparent as she gazed through the window pane.

These thoughts did not reassure Detective Reynard as he slipped past the house in the darkness, making his way towards the hospital down the paved roads which connected the outbuildings to the main one.

"Hey! Hey, you!"

Someone was shouting at him and he turned around to see a figure in a bright yellow jacket, only a few yards away. It was pointless to run, he was old and fat, and besides, he could just say he was out for a walk. It was pretty much public property, after all.

He turned around and saw it was a familiar face. It was the same guard he had seen the day of the murder. The one who had shown him the security tape.

"Oh, it's you," he said, approaching with his flashlight. He had dimmed it while he snuck up on Reynard.

"Yes, I'm back. Sorry if I startled you. Detective Reynard. I'm trying to get a feel for this place, what it was like that night when Gertrude was escaping," he said, lying.

"I see... So I guess you haven't had any luck finding her yet?"

The security guard didn't know that they'd received a call from her that day. Reynard played this to his advantage.

"No, we haven't found any sign of her. It makes me wonder... Nah, it's too unlikely..."

They were walking towards the hospital now and the security guard looked at him with curiosity.

"What is it? What are you thinking?"

He looked at him carefully.

"What's your name, kid?"

"Bruce."

"Well, Bruce, if I tell you this, I'm letting you in on a secret that's part of this investigation - you mention it to anyone, and I mean anyone, I could be in a lot of trouble."

"I won't say anything, I swear."

"Alright. I haven't even told my partner this theory yet. It's kinda out there, you know. But... Well, I was thinking - that day when she escaped - she was hiding here in plain sight. She knows this place really well, right? Well, what if she never left? Just stashed the car in somebody's garage or left it with the keys inside running for somebody to steal, and then she just came back here and hunkered down in the hospital basement somewhere. Do you think it's possible?"

He thought about this for a minute.

"No, probably not. Someone would have spotted her by now, I'm pretty sure. We've been doing extra checks down there since the murder and we've cleared out any potential hiding places."

Pausing, he looked down at the ground, furrowing his brow. Then he looked up at Reynard with an enthusiastic expression on his face.

"Hey! There's also the sub basement. Me and the other guards, we don't go down there. Not after the stories we've heard. It's supposed to be ancient - one of the few remaining parts of the original structure that still exists within the main building. But it's infested with rats, water-damaged, not to mention flooded half the time. Same with Century Manor, that old mansion back there. It's liable to fall down one day so we don't go inside. Too much of a safety risk. The two are supposed to be connected by the sub basement, though."

"I see. Well, maybe you could show me how to get down to the sub basement for myself? So I can take a look?"

The kid looked really freaked out.

"Why the hell do you want to go down there? It's all locked up. And it's not safe."

The guard hesitated for a moment before adding, "They told us not to go down there. No matter what. They said it's really, really dangerous down there."

"Who told you not to go down there?"

"The other guys who... I'm not supposed to talk about it, really. But there's these other guys who work here who are on leave right now. They've been down there before, multiple times. There's been some... escaped patients... Things like that. They could tell you more than I can."

"I might ask to get in touch with them, if you have their number. But I'd really like to go down there tonight."

"Why do you want to go down there so bad, anyways? Most people would want to stay the hell away from a place like that. I know I'm terrified of it. I have nightmares sometimes that the boss sends me down there to fetch a lost patient - I get attacked by rats and they eat my face. In the dream, that is."

I had a dream about it too, he thought but once again could not say.

He *knew* somehow that there was something down there. It was something about that day when Mertzek had taken him in the wheelchair, how his hand hovered over the button for the basement, as if considering taking him down there instead of where he was supposed to.

And what was in the basement? Nothing but boiler rooms, storage rooms, pantries, and patient records from what he had seen. But perhaps there was something beneath that. A place where Mertzek took his most special patients. The ones who disappeared. A few of them each week, gone missing never to return. He had seen it when he was a patrolman, then when he became a detective in the Missing Persons Division. It had stopped for a little while, but then got worse again - the problem of the missing patients from St. Daniel's. Everyone said the patients just fled the city, or the country, but that was far too simple of an explanation. Too many of them disappeared permanently, never to be found.

Mertzek was rotten, it was just up to Reynard to prove it. And he was realizing that all of this was connected somehow. He had investigated those disappeared patients in the past, when he worked in the missing persons department. Now was his chance to finally solve that riddle once and for all.

"I just have a hunch," was all he said to the kid. And he left it at that. He was very thankful the guard didn't ask to see his badge. That would have been an issue.

The security guard held the hatch open for Reynard and he slid into the hole, finding the top rung of the ladder with his foot, then carefully climbing downwards into the darkness below.

"You know I can't wait here for long, right? And I can't just leave this hatch open. My boss would kill me."

Reynard looked up at him, surveying the filthy basement storage room where he was expecting the guard to wait. It was a good thing he had run into the guy, in retrospect, since he would have had no idea how to find this hidden ladder in the main building's lower level which led into the sub basement.

"Give me fifteen minutes. If I'm not back by then, call the police station and ask for Lieutenant Snead at Homicide. Tell him everything I told you and tell him to come quickly with backup. If I'm right about this - then I'm gonna need support down there. And lots of it."

"Are you sure you should be doing this alone? Why don't you have anybody with you?"

"Budget cuts. It's just a hunch, kid. I'll be fine - and if by some odd chance I'm not, you're gonna get somebody over here to help me. Right?"

The kid nodded and he climbed downwards into the blackened tunnel.

"Be careful," he called down to him. "There are rats down there. And... Other things... And remember, you won't have any cell service or radio signal down there. The concrete is too thick!"

When he got down to the bottom of the ladder, Detective Reynard shone his flashlight beam around and saw a terrifying dark corridor surrounding him. There were doors lining each stone-brick wall. Thick doors made of steel, riveted every few inches as if this were an old prison of some kind. There were slits just big enough for hands to reach through at eye level, presumably for guards to look in on the patients back when this place was actually functional.

This place being functional - that idea brought with it a horrifying array of mental images. Hands reaching out from those mailslot-sized holes in the doors, reaching out desperately for freedom, for air, for food and water, but more than that, for love and for comfort from someone, *anyone.* He imagined their wailing cries echoing down these dark corridors as they wasted away down here.

"I can't believe they actually kept people down here," he whispered to himself, as if afraid to wake the ghosts that surely resided down in this ancient place. *If not here, then where?*

He crept slowly down the dark, stone floored hallway, past the doors with dark rooms hidden inside. After peering into one of them with his flashlight he found he could not bring himself to investigate any others, his heart skipping a beat when a rat moved away from the beam of his flashlight, its red eyes reflecting like mirrors in the dim glow. More rats and mice scampered past his feet and he saw cockroaches and spiders as well, their webs hanging low across the corridor at times, getting caught in his hair as he travelled through the tunnel.

The air was moist and cool down in the sub basement, too dark to see anything without his flashlight. He tried to shine it upon every surface as he searched desperately for clues, but he had no idea what it was he was looking for.

On and on, the doors went. He rounded a bend, being careful to keep track of his location and his movement. This place was known to be a labyrinth, and he had barely scratched the surface of it.

Suddenly it occurred to him that he could spend all day down in this place and never find a thing, even if it existed. He was searching for the metaphorical needle in a haystack.

What if I just called out, he wondered to himself. *What if I just shouted down here in these echoing underground corridors and waited to see what answers back?*

He shuddered at the thought. Something almost certainly would respond, he felt in his gut. And he didn't want to know what it would be. Reynard had never believed in ghosts, not really. But he had seen the odd special on Discovery channel or the odd thing online like the pictures of the ghost in the window at Century Manor. Those images seemed all too real down here, wandering these dark, haunted hallways beneath the sanatorium. It seemed like if there was a place where those things existed, this would definitely be it.

As if on cue, he heard something. The sound of someone clearing their throat, far up ahead. It echoed down the stone corridor and turned Reynard's blood ice cold in the dark.

He felt a chill run down his spine and tried to will his feet to move once again but they would not.

There was someone down there with him.

16: No Pain, No Gain

Reynard was suddenly very glad he had not called out into the darkness. But now he had a decision to make. There were two options. He either turned back now and got help, or he continued forward with his flashlight turned off.

His eyes would adjust to the light - or lack thereof. But he could not risk being spotted if someone was down here. They could sneak up on him too easily. He could use the light sparingly, but he would have to move in darkness, in order to conceal his presence down here.

The decision was strangely easy to make. He switched his flashlight off and the tunnel was plunged into utter blackness.

With that, he continued moving forward, picturing the tunnel ahead of him as he had seen it with the light on a moment before. The after-image hung before his vision and he managed to picture it clearly for a while before losing sight of it. There was no way he would be able to see without the light, he realized. It was so dark down here that he couldn't see his hand in front of his face from an inch away, even after letting his eyes adjust for several minutes.

There was a sound again, someone talking to themself. It was coming from one of the hallways up ahead, leading to the left. He was counting them as he went, trying desperately not to lose track. Suddenly it was becoming more and more obvious why this section of the hospital was locked up with thick chains and padlocks. If a child or a group of urban-exploring teenagers wandered down into the sub basement they could easily become lost and would never find their way out of this dark place. However, it also made it an excellent place for someone to hide.

Escape from the Asylum / Jordan Grupe

He kept walking towards the sound, now constant, of someone talking to themselves in low tones. It sounded like a man was whispering his own thoughts to himself, talking through some problem.

"...if only... But, no... Ugh, I should have just made it a bit narrower..."

Reynard was only catching bits of pieces of the man's speech, but it made it possible for him to locate him, at least. But now he had made several turns and was trying hard to keep them all in his mind for the trip back. He had to remember not only the lefts and rights, but also how many hallways were in between.

Finally, he came to a doorway with a dim light glowing from the base of the closed door. The voice of the man was coming from inside, and Reynard realized suddenly that it sounded familiar. It sounded like Mertzek.

"Ah, now that is a simple yet elegant solution," he was saying to himself, standing in front of a small chalkboard. He was admiring a chemical formula of some sort, by the looks of it.

The room was full of laboratory equipment. A workbench was covered in beakers and vials, scales and a tabletop centrifuge. Most of the tools and equipment looked old and in disrepair, but there were a few newer pieces as well.

Reynard glanced in through the window at the top of the door, the same as the ones where he had come in - just a mailslot-sized hole where guards could check in on the patients under their watch. It seemed this whole floor had been dedicated to housing patients at one time, long in the distant past. Such numbers were unheard of recently - they were emptying out the mental hospitals' inpatients programs nowadays. There had been a huge purge decades before and now only the most severe mental health cases were hospitalized. The rest were treated as outpatients or fell between the cracks in the system - more often than not, sadly, it was the latter of the two. His wife had been a social worker, which was why he knew this more acutely than others.

Escape from the Asylum / Jordan Grupe

Mertzek stood admiring his work for a few more moments then spun around suddenly. Reynard ducked so as not to be seen, and believed he got out of sight just in time.

But suddenly it was quiet from inside the room. Mertzek was no longer speaking to himself. It was still and silent down in the sub basement of the mental hospital. The only sound was the scurrying of mice and rats and the drip drip drip of water splashing down into a puddle somewhere nearby. A leaky pipe, perhaps.

Reynard felt exposed. He had told the kid to call for backup in fifteen minutes. How long had it been? It felt like hours, but he was too terrified at that moment to look at the time.

Once again, he had two options. He could go into the room and try to arrest Mertzek - *On what charge?* His mind couldn't help but ask. *And you're not even a cop anymore, remember? You don't have your badge, and you don't have your gun.*

It was true. He was essentially defenseless against Mertzek. If the man had a weapon or simply overpowered him, he could die down there. If only Lieutenant Snead hadn't listened to this mad scientist doctor - he had been gaming them all from the beginning.

"Reynard, is that you?"

The voice came from the other side of the door, sounding almost delighted.

"You know I can see your feet under the door, right?"

He giggled and Reynard actually slapped himself on the forehead. *How could he be so stupid?* Clearly the drugs were still affecting him, whatever the doctor had doped him with. Now it was all beginning to make sense - no wonder the blood tests at the hospital had come back negative. They were testing him for drugs which were known to them - cocaine, heroin, GHB, Lysergic Acid, cannabinoids, and a long list of pharmaceuticals and other illicit substances - your standard Tox Screen, in other words - but they couldn't test for things that they didn't know existed.

Escape from the Asylum / Jordan Grupe

Mertzek was making his own supply of chemical weapons. His own brand of demented pharmaceuticals. And Reynard had been his unwitting guinea pig.

That was why he had this lab down in the sub basement. To make his own drugs.

"You caught me, Reynard. Good job, really impressive! Too bad you're not a police officer anymore. I heard they took your badge and gun - just like in those cop movies when the leading man is getting a bit too headstrong. How thrilling! What do you have out there to defend yourself? A bread knife?"

He still didn't speak. He didn't want to give Mertzek the satisfaction of knowing it was really him.

"Cat got your tongue? Or is it a rat?"

Reynard couldn't help look over his shoulder at the mention of rats. They were everywhere, brushing up against his legs occasionally and sniffing at his exposed skin.

"Well, I'll speak for the both of us," Mertzek said tauntingly. "See, when I found out you were suspended, I knew you'd be coming for me. I didn't expect you to find me so fast, I'll admit. But I knew you'd find this place sooner or later. That's why I came prepared."

The unmistakable sound of a semi-automatic pistol being cocked could be heard from the other side of the door. And then a scream.

"Run!" Someone yelled, their voice unfamiliar. It was a woman.

A shot rang out and another scream rang through the echoing corridors from inside the room. Reynard stole one last quick glance through the peephole and saw something he had missed the first time.

On the floor in the corner of the room, a woman was chained up and on all fours. She was filthy, her hair a tangled mat - a prisoner being kept inside a dog kennel. The whites of her eyes

Escape from the Asylum / Jordan Grupe

were barely visible in the torchlight but he saw her, and he locked her features in his memory, telling himself he would not let her die down there with this madman.

And then another shot rang out and he ran away from the door as fast as he could, flashlight in hand to guide his way.

Counting the doors and hallways as he ran, he was distracted for a moment by the laughter of Doctor Mertzek in the tunnel behind him. Another shot echoed through the tunnel and he nearly lost track of where he was.

But then it didn't matter anymore, because the voice of Bruce, the security guard who had helped him down there, could be heard calling to him from above.

"Hey, I'm calling the cops now! It's been fifteen minutes, dude! If you're still alive down there can you fucking say something already!?"

"Hang on! I'm coming," Reynard shouted back.

When he got back up the ladder, he was panting and out of breath, completely exhausted.

"What the hell happened down there," the guard asked, looking worried. "I thought I heard gunshots!"

"He's got somebody in a fucking cage down there. He's doing experiments on her. I'm calling it in."

Reynard took out his phone and looked at the screen. At the top it read: No signal.

"We never get any service down here. Too much concrete. C'mon, let's go outside and get some air," the guard said, shutting the hatch behind him. "What the hell was down there with you?"

After calling in for backup, they waited outside in the brisk night air for reinforcements to arrive. The whole time Reynard could only imagine the shit he was going to be in. But also he thought of the seconds ticking away as the doctor prepared his escape down in the sub basement.

Reynard looked at his watch again and again, the time stretching on and on forever.

Finally a couple cop cars arrived, pulling into the parking lot lackadaisically with their red and blue lights flashing. He flagged them down and they got out and came over to talk to him.

"Snead said we need to wait for SWAT," one of the uniformed officers told him. "He's pissed with you by the way."

"Well, he can be pissed with me all he wants if it means we make an arrest."

"You're suspended - so if anyone is making an arrest it'll be us, not you. What the hell were you doing down there anyways? I thought this woman was up north somewhere."

Bruce, the security guard, shot Reynard a quick look, showing that he realized he'd been lied to earlier. Reynard felt a pang of guilt for a moment, mostly for having been caught. In his line of work lying was part of the job description.

"I thought you hadn't heard from her yet," the guard said, annoyance creeping into his voice. "That's why you were going down there, you said. To look for her."

"Just following up on a lead," Reynard replied, hoping that would satisfy both of them. Judging by the looks on their faces, it didn't.

The SWAT team arrived with Snead a little while later. The older Lieutenant put on a kevlar vest and handed one to Reynard.

"Am I going down with you?"

"You bet your ass you are," Snead said. "You have to show us where this secret torture chamber slash chemical weapons lab is, Reynard. Meanwhile I've got a car at the doctor's house checking up on him, making sure he isn't there. I sure hope for your sake you're right about this."

The look on the old man's face said it all. He would be allowed in the tunnels to show them the way, but that would be the extent of it. He wouldn't be getting his Detective badge back anytime soon.

Reynard showed them exactly back to the place where Mertzek had been holding the woman captive, leading them through the blackened basement corridors filled with cobwebs. The adrenaline was palpable as every corner was cleared, searching for the doctor and his patient.

But they found nothing. No bullet holes, no equipment, no cage, and certainly no prisoners of a mad scientist doctor doing experiments beneath the hospital.

It was like none of it had ever happened.

An hour or so later, after the SWAT team had packed up and gone home and the asylum's basements were deathly silent once again, a phone began to ring on the other side of town, in the apartment of an off-duty security guard. It was the fifth or sixth time it had rung, from the same private number, and it had gone through to voicemail each time. But this time, the recipient of the call picked up the phone.

"It's four-thirty in the morning, who the hell is this?"

"It's Bruce, over at the hospital."

"Bruce??? What do you want, man? I'm trying to sleep. I'm on personal leave, remember?"

"I know, but you said to call if anything happens down in the sub basement, right?"

The guard bolted upright in his bed. "Yeah. So?"

"Well, some crazy shit just happened in the sub basement. I think you need to get over here right now."

Escape from the Asylum / Jordan Grupe

17: Actions Speak Louder Than Words

"What line of work are you in, Allison?" Reynard asked. They were drinking coffee in her hotel room. He had brought her breakfast. A bagel with cream cheese and lox.

She took a small bite and set it down immediately.

"Not hungry?"

She shook her head.

"I'm not working right now," she said, her mouth full with the small bite which she chewed slowly and deliberately.

"But you did, right? I remember Jim telling me you were a journalist?"

Allison nodded, then picked up her coffee and took a long sip from it, washing down the bagel, cream cheese, and salmon. For a moment it looked as if she was gagging on it, but choked down the bit with watering eyes.

"Investigative journalism. I did several expose articles - a few of them got picked up by other news outlets."

"Oh, wow. It sounds like you must have been really good. Didn't Jim say you were a… Feature Writer, that's it! Sounds pretty impressive."

"I was. But it was time to call it quits after twenty years. It was all getting too stressful."

"That's funny, because I remember Jim saying you never wanted to quit. That you loved it so much and then one day you just kinda got tired of it. What was that, about a year ago?"

"Eight months."

"So you quit or they let you go?"

Dell shifted uncomfortably in his seat.

"Hey, Reynard, this was just supposed to be a friendly visit. What's with all the questions?"

"We're still working a case, aren't we? I thought this could be relevant."

Dell pulled him aside and whispered to him angrily.

"*I'm* working on a case. *You're* suspended. I shouldn't have even brought you here after that mess at the hospital. I can't believe I let you talk me into this."

"You're right, Dell, I'm sorry, Allison. Just one last question, though. Did you quit or did they let you go?"

Allison glared at him.

"It was a mutual decision," she said, practically spitting the words.

"I'm telling you, Dell. There's something going on here."

"What the hell are you talking about Reynard? Are you gonna explain to me why you badgered your dead partner's fucking widow like that?"

They were back in Dell's car now, parked outside the hotel where Allison was staying.

"There's something going on she's not telling us, Dell. I know it sounds crazy - I know I must seem crazy to you right now - but you have to believe me."

"What do you think she isn't telling us, Reynard? She's been up front about everything so far."

"Or she's been lying from the beginning, Dell. Since a year ago."

"A year ago? What are you talking about?"

"You ever see those movies where the twins switch places? The Parent Trap? You know what I'm talking about, right?"

"I hope you're not saying what I think you're saying. That you believed that woman on the phone when she told you she wasn't Gertrude."

Reynard didn't reply, he just let Dell sit with the idea for a moment.

"What the hell was up with the bagel and lox in there? You insisted on getting that on the way over and she hated it. You said that was her favourite thing in the fucking world according to Jim, and she hated it."

"Yeah, up until about a year ago that was what he'd buy her for breakfast every weekend. We'd swing by his place sometimes to drop it off. Then all of a sudden she didn't like it anymore."

"Well, people's tastes change."

"True, people's tastes do change. Alright, let's just forget about it for now. You're probably right."

Dell stared at him for a few seconds before relenting.

"Okay, let's say *you're* right. Let's say it is true - despite the kid obviously protesting in the background on the call. Let's say they switched - let's say it happened a year ago when the attack occurred - right before the face tattoo we're all using as a reference to tell them apart. The cops arrest the wrong twin somehow and they ignore her protests when she says she's not Gertrude - because she looks crazy - maybe her sister feeds her some LCD before tattooing her forehead. Far-fetched, but I'll buy it for our purposes at the moment.

Escape from the Asylum / Jordan Grupe

"She spends months in jail and almost a year in the asylum. Then she manages to escape by *killing a security guard* and getting away. Don't you fucking get it, man? Either way she's a *murderer*. Not only that - she's Gertrude. The whole thing is a lie or a delusion. It's obvious. The doctors would have noticed having a sane person in their care. They would have realized right away she wasn't ill! My sister is a nurse at one of these places, you think she can't tell the difference between somebody who's really sick and somebody who's not? And don't you think her fucking husband would have noticed? He was a detective, wasn't he?"

A detective who barely spent any time with his wife because he was too busy with the job. Still, Reynard didn't have a good answer for that one that wouldn't come off sounding petty and argumentative. Dell was right, after all. It was far-fetched. Maybe even impossible.

"So if it really was true, and Gertrude somehow managed to convince everyone she was Allison, including Jim, her coworkers, her boss - and not only that but *Allison* managed to remain unnoticed as a sane person in the mental institute for almost a year - I mean, come on! It's just not possible. You know that. The simplest explanation is usually the right one, and Reynard, that's about the furthest thing from simple I've ever heard."

"You're right, Dell. Simplest is usually best. Except nothing about murder is simple. People go to unimaginable lengths to try and cover their tracks, to try and preemptively figure out how the police will catch them - assuming they're smart and it's pre-planned. And this escape is as pre-planned as they come."

He had just finished telling himself it was probably impossible and yet here he was pushing the issue further. For some reason he just couldn't stop himself.

"So why did she kill the guard?"

"I don't know yet. But she might have had a reason. And she might not be lying about who she says she is - that's the more important bit for if and when we catch her."

"So you intend to keep pursuing this? I don't know, Reynard. This all sounds like a very long leap to me. If it's all the same to you, I'm out. If you want to do your own thing and try to prove it, go for it, just don't tell Snead you had my blessing. Because, frankly, you don't. I'm gonna drop you back off at your place. Snead is gonna give me shit as it is for bringing you up here today. You better believe one of those cops inside the hotel is gonna be talking about this."

"I appreciate it, Dell. And I'm sorry if I get you into any shit with Snead. But listen, please don't mention any of this to anybody, okay? Let's just keep it between you and me for now, until I have something solid. I'll keep you up to date - even though you don't want me to."

"Fine. Just don't call me on my work cell. I don't need Snead listening in to *that* conversation," Dell said, backing out of the parking space in the hotel parking lot. He pulled out onto the street and drove in the direction of Reynard's place.

He tried not to fall asleep but it was difficult during the drive. His eyes kept slipping closed and he was nodding off despite his best efforts. It had been a couple days since he'd had a good night's sleep. But there was no time for it now. There was too much to do.

His eyes snapped awake as the car came to a stop outside the house.

"Alright, here you go, buddy. Listen, I'm sure you'll get your badge back soon, it's just policy and procedure bullshit. All they need is a clean bill of health from the hospital and that should come through any day now. You went through all those tests and everything was probably negative, right? So that should be a good thing! Just try to look on the bright side."

Reynard winced internally, thinking about what the doctor had told him at the hospital regarding his liver. He got out of the car and closed the door behind him, looking in at Dell through the open window.

"Yeah, you're right. I'll just put my feet up here and try to catch up on my sleep until I hear from Snead. Thanks for indulging me today, Dell. I appreciate it."

"Anytime. And hey, I'll let you know if we hear anything about Gertrude's whereabouts."

He nodded and Dell drove off, his clean, polished black car sparkling bright enough to hurt Reynard's eyes. *The sun is too damn bright today*, he thought to himself. He never wore sunglasses but he wished he had a pair today.

It was okay, though. He wouldn't be outside for long.

Taking out his cell phone, he dialled the number for the Yellow Tree Cab Company, one of the local taxi services.

"Hello, can I have a cab at 188 West Thirtieth Street, please?"

"And where are you heading?"

"Investigation Weekly's office, here in town. I believe they're on Main and Sherman."

"No problem, we'll be there right away."

He hung up the call and stood in front of his house, waiting for the cab to arrive. He wasn't supposed to drive, but nobody ever said anything about a taxi.

Escape from the Asylum / Jordan Grupe

18: Don't Quit Your Day Job

"I don't know how comfortable I feel talking about all this. I mean, she's the victim here, right? Why are you even asking about her job history?"

"It's all part of the investigation," said Reynard. "I can't be any more specific than that." He'd gotten upstairs using an old police ID. It wasn't a badge, but still looked official enough that no one questioned it. And it had his face on it, showing him in uniform. "Well, we had to let her go, frankly."

"So it was a dismissal. And can I ask what the cause was?"

"Her writing. She was working on something great, then all of a sudden... It was just starting to slip. To be honest, for the last three or four months she worked here it was all unusable. As good as she was, she lost the magic. It was kinda strange. She was one of my best writers, then suddenly she just lost that spark. The writing was fine - no errors, meticulous, driving to a conclusion, all that - but it had no... soul. No fire. And Allison's writing always had that. She was a big reason people subscribed to us. Our numbers took a hit since she left and we still get letters to the editor asking when she'll be back... she was a draw."

"What exactly *was* she working on before her writing started to drop off? You said she was working on something intriguing then suddenly she changed course?"

"She was doing an expose on that mental health facility. St. Daniel's, up on the escarpment. The one that overlooks the city. It was gonna be her first really impressive local piece - usually she did more national news. But she picked that topic herself and said whatever she was researching wasn't going to just be local news. It was going to be huge."

"Any idea what it was about?"

"She wouldn't say. Just that it was gonna be some big groundbreaking thing. Actually I was pretty disappointed when she told me it didn't pan out the way she wanted. I was excited to read it - just as a fan of her work. With her I rarely ever had to edit anything. I didn't dare cut a word of her articles, either. Everything she wrote made it in."

"Do you have any early drafts? Anything I could look at from that time period?"

He looked at his computer screen and pulled up his email. "She was pretty secretive about stuff. I had to pull teeth to get anything out of her most of the time. Ummm, let's see... No, nothing from that article. It was all in-person conversations. She never liked to talk over email about her projects, either. She was always worried about getting hacked."

"And who has her old laptop? The one with all these files on it?"

"Allison does. She always used her own device. She said the ones we supplied were crap - I can't argue there. We don't have the budget for decent machines and most writers have their own."

Great, Reynard thought to himself. *No chance I'm gonna get to read that. Unless it was taken as evidence in the house search.*

"Can I just ask you one more favor? Could you send me a couple of those unusable articles? I just want to check them out."

"You'd have to promise not to let anybody else see them. If I found them on some other website, I'd know how they got there."

"Don't worry. I just want to read them. I won't share them with anybody. Just between you and me, I don't think it'll amount to anything, but we have to cover our bases."

The guy thought about it for a few long moments and Reynard was sure he'd say no, but then he nodded. "Alright, what's your email? I'll see if I can find some of the ones she sent me. I can promise you, though, they don't make for very interesting reading."

That evening he read through a few of the articles that Allison had written nearly a year before. Like the editor had told him, they weren't terrible. Just lacking any real emotion or heart. It was just the facts, laid out with a clarity and preciseness similar to the writing of someone who does technical books for a living.

She had done one about the Great Pacific Garbage Patch and a new effort to remove waste from it, and another article was about the poaching of venus fly traps in South Carolina. That one started off well, but then he was soon falling asleep while reading it, bored out of his mind and bogged down by details.

He went online and found some of Allison's writing from over a year before, paying the extra fee with his credit card after maxing out the number of articles available for free. Pretty soon he had forgotten all about the case and was lost in an expose about a corrupt television evangelist based in Florida. After some more research he saw that his career had been ruined by the piece and he was now facing legal charges.

The difference between the articles from the last year and from those the years prior was impossible to deny. Her earlier writing was crisp and thought-provoking. Where the newer articles were bulging with numbers and facts, these older articles brought such numbers to life with anecdotes and descriptions of conversations, places and events that made him feel as if he were really there.

Pretty soon he had read a half dozen of these older articles and found that it was nearly 4AM. He had been completely lost in the writings of Allison Paulson. And yet her newer work was completely unreadable and unpublishable. How was that possible? *How could the editor not see it,* he wondered to himself. *These are two different women.*

He realized he was buying it, at least for the time being. It was still a theory, but it was now his working theory. They had switched at the time of the attack a year prior - when Gertrude had marred Allison for life by tattooing her forehead. She had tried to make her look insane, and she had succeeded. Perhaps she had drugged her, in the same way Mertzek had done to Reynard. He was suddenly sympathizing with her more and more - the *real* Allison, not the psychopathic killer currently being granted police protection at a fancy hotel.

He tried to piece together the events of a couple days prior, now nearing the end of that crucial 48 hour window when it becomes much more difficult to find a killer. And his suspect had just changed entirely, as had his whole investigation. Except his murder suspect was still the same, he realized. Despite everything it was still an undeniable fact that whoever escaped from the hospital killed a security guard to get away.

His partner's words echoed in his mind: *Don't you fucking get it, man? Either way she's a murderer.*

If she was innocent why would she kill the man just for doing his job? It didn't make sense. She could have just as easily slipped into the woods and hidden from sight just after leaving the unit, at 3 PM. She could have hidden until nightfall, then stolen a car without hurting anyone. It was the biggest hole in his version of events. He tried to reconcile an innocent woman killing a security guard in the brutal fashion he had seen and just couldn't do it.

Suddenly his whole theory seemed to crumble before his eyes. He didn't know what to believe anymore. What if the whole thing *was* just a lie told by an escaped killer to throw him off her trail. If it was, it certainly was working.

Exhaustion hit Reynard suddenly and he found his eyelids closing of their own accord. He hadn't slept much the last couple days. As his eyes wandered the pages of text in reports of the crime scenes and phone call transcriptions, he found himself unable to concentrate.

And so, as the sun was just beginning to come up, Reynard wandered upstairs to bed and fell down on his mattress like a sack of bricks, falling unconscious almost immediately once his head hit the pillow. He slept well, but his dreams were no better than the last time. This time they were far, far worse.

19: Opening Pandora's Box

Reynard was dreaming that he was strapped to a table in an underground laboratory. Not just any underground lab, but the one he had seen Mertzek inside of. The one where he had glimpsed a woman being held prisoner inside a cage the size of a dog kennel.

He turned his head and saw she was still there, bleeding from the nose, bruised and emaciated, looking like she was on the verge of death. A wretched, starving corpse just barely hanging onto the last thread of life, in order to tell him one thing.

"You left me here to die," she croaked.

Seeing her up close he could imagine what it must feel like to be in that confined space, unable to stretch your legs out no matter how badly you wanted to. Unable to stand up and unable to move. It made him cringe and shudder with a terrible feeling.

"Why didn't you help me?"

He tried to speak but he found his mouth was gagged. His feet were tied tightly down and so were his wrists. His heartbeat was speeding up, going faster and faster as he struggled to breathe.

"Yes, Detective. Why didn't you help this poor woman? Why didn't you *protect* her? Isn't that your job, to serve and to *protect*?"

The snake-like voice was familiar and in this darkened space he recognized there was only one person it could belong to. Mertzek, the mad psychiatrist.

"All this time hunting for a fugitive, sending all those officers on that wild goose chase up north... And she's been here right in front of you this whole time, Detective."

He looked down at the cage again to see it was Gertrude's face inside the cage - only perhaps it wasn't Gertrude, perhaps it was Allison - a blue-inked tattoo stamped upon her face like an animal being sent off from the slaughterhouse.

"Nobody is going to believe you. You know that, right?" the woman with flesh sloughing from her ruined face asked from within the cage. And now it was impossible to tell them apart. How could you without faces?

Fingerprints. The thought flew in and out of his dream-sick mind like a bird gathering twigs and leaves for a nest. Flimsy scraps of debris and detritus that would eventually create something sturdy and whole.

Reynard's mind was suddenly panicking and racing, his thoughts coming quickly as he tried to figure out what to do. But he still didn't realize he was dreaming. If he had he would have tried to snap awake at that instant. It didn't help that he had been drugged with a heavy dose of sedatives.

A light pinch like a bee-sting could be felt at the base of his skull and then a strange sensation like something digging and burrowing beneath his skin back there. Like an insect crawling towards his brain-stem.

"Ah, just like that. Perfect," whispered Mertzek in his ear.

He looked over and saw the woman in the cage was now dead. Her skin was beginning to rot and maggots were crawling across her skeletal face. She was still trapped there standing on all fours - even in death - frozen in that position like a taxidermied dog.

Her rotting face had millipedes going in and out of her eye sockets and her jaw was exposed in places, but still it opened and she spoke.

"You," she said bitterly. "This is all your fault. You did this to me."

When he awoke, the whole world was different.

20: I'll Take a Rain Check

His cell phone was ringing from the bedside table and it rattled with vibration as he struggled to grab it blindly.

When he picked it up in his hand, the screen was hazy and blurred, difficult to make out. But then he saw it was a private number calling. "Reynard here," he said, just as a sharp pain like a needle pierced through his temple. The old detective bit his lip to try and stifle a scream, but only half-managed to do so.

"Hello, is this Detective Reynard?"

"Yes, speaking. Who's this?"

"My name is Marcy Stern. I'm a Recreational Therapist at St. Daniel's Mental Health Facility."

"Oh. And can I ask what this is about?"

"I'd like to speak with you about Gertrude Remier. There's something important I think may be getting overlooked. I don't want to say more on the phone. Can you come here to speak with me in my office?"

"Well, actually, I'm not assigned to the case anymore. I can give you the number of Detective Dell - you should talk to him now."

She lowered her voice discreetly. "No, that's not going to be possible. Please, you have to trust me on this. I need to speak with you directly. Nobody else. I don't trust anyone else."

He couldn't resist the temptation to hear the woman out. Despite his lack of officiality at the moment, this was sounding promising to the investigation. "Alright, I'll be there."

He hung up the phone and managed to get dressed, the headache abating a bit once he got in the shower. One thing was for sure, he needed to get some painkillers. He would need to stop by the drug store on the way in. Suddenly he didn't trust any of the open bottles in his house. Not after what Mertzek had done to him.

What had Mertzek done to him? The thought occurred once again, but he brushed it aside. *Was Mertzek still doing something to him?*

He got in his car and drove fast towards the hospital, stopping by the pharmacy on the way. The bright fluorescent lights burnt his eyes and almost doubled him over in sudden blinding pain, but he managed to get through it and pay for the largest bottle of codeine-tylenol pills he could buy.

He popped four of them into his mouth and dry-swallowed them before he had even left the store. The checkout girl looked at him like he was an addict of some sort. *Maybe I am.*

Flying out of the parking lot in the old black Crown Victoria, he smelled burnt rubber and realized people were staring at him from the sidewalks. Ignoring them, he made his way to the asylum. The old building on the escarpment which was the source of so many local legends, and so much personal anguish in his own life. His mother had died while hospitalized there, he remembered. Although the details of it escaped him. All he remembered about it was sadness and despair, wishing he could go home and stay away from that pale-yellow-walled place forever. With its strange cleaning-product stench mixed with B.O. and bad cafeteria food.

People around town liked to talk excitedly about the place - telling stories to each other of spectres and apparitions. Ghost-hunters and online sleuths took to visiting the ancient, crumbling mansion at the back of the property. Breaking in, trying to catch a glimpse of these phantoms.

Reynard had never seen anything like that himself, either at the hospital or anywhere else, but he had heard enough stories from credible people to know that such things were possible. He'd even seen pictures of the place online, in passing. But such things could be easily altered with computer software.

One officer he knew well had worked at the asylum as a security guard once upon a time. They had been partners for a little while in the street crimes division and he'd regaled Reynard with tale after terrifying tale from the place. He told him how the door to the old mansion at the back of the property would swing open as he walked past sometimes, especially late at night. It would be closed and padlocked tightly shut, then he would look over and would see it suddenly ajar, the gaping black darkness from within peering at him, and the feeling of something else watching too.

He'd told him how once during the winter he had walked past the field outside that mansion on a night patrol and seen someone standing there in the snow, staring at him. It was 3AM and made no sense for someone to be standing out there, so he called out to them.

"Security, identify yourself!" he shouted, but there was no answer.

"Security!" he yelled again, but there was nothing. "Hey, you gotta leave. You can't stay here."

That was when the black silhouette had begun to walk away. It went straight through a chain-link fence nearby as if it didn't exist. Then it walked off into the trees, disappearing. When the guy looked for footprints in the morning, there were none. The snow was crisp and fresh, despite no more having fallen.

Reynard had heard stories like that, and others, about the place on the mountain they called *The Sanatorium*. He didn't like going there, especially with his own history, new and old, but it seemed there was no choice at the moment. He had to follow the clues - and that meant going back to the one place in the world he was most afraid of.

He parked in the lot and a woman came over to him as he was walking towards the front door.

"Oh, hey," she said. "I'm the one who called you. Marcy - Rec Therapist for Forensics."

Escape from the Asylum / Jordan Grupe

"Nice to meet you. Detective Reynard, Homicide." He stuck out his hand to shake but then remembered he wasn't supposed to do that anymore and retracted it awkwardly.

"Come on into my office, I don't want to talk openly about this. Not when there's so many other people around."

Reynard didn't see anybody else nearby, but agreed. Whatever made her comfortable sharing with him.

"Did you know Gertrude well," he asked, as they walked towards the doors.

"Yes, I mean, I know they said she did horrible things but I can hardly believe it myself. She was a sweetheart - it didn't seem like she had a hostile bone in her body. I just feel so bad for her. The poor thing had so many issues, but she didn't like to open up to many people."

"Did she open up to you?"

"In a way, she did. As Recreational Therapists we're viewed a bit differently by the patients, I think. They don't see us as part of the healthcare team as much, per say, and more as their friends. At least, some of them do."

"I'm struggling to make sense of her behaviour. She has no history of violence aside from the attack against her sister, which was of course the whole reason she was committed, and the damage she did to herself. Why, all of a sudden, does she hide in the shadows for the day, just to kill this poor, innocent security guard? Especially when she could have just left much more easily during the day. Was there any indication of that sort of homicidal tendency in her disposition? Or do you know if she had a vendetta of some sort against this security guard in particular?"

"No - and it doesn't add up for me, either. To be honest, even the incident with her sister didn't completely mesh with what I saw of her," Marcy was saying to him quietly as they got on the elevator. She hit the "B" button and it began to descend. "She wasn't violent. She didn't display any of the tendencies I'd associate with a psychotic, once we had her medicated."

"What if she stopped taking her medication?"

She shook her head.

"Impossible. The pills were always taken with a nurse witnessing. Nurses give a lot of meds in liquid form, so that people can't pocket them - hide them under their tongue or in their cheek. The pharmacy makes them special that way for us."

"Interesting. So there's no chance she was getting out of it somehow?"

"I highly doubt it. You have to remember, we're dealing with a dangerous population here. We have to look out for our own safety as well as the safety of the other patients. Back when I started, we used to use physical restraints - limb holders, straight-jackets, hand mitts to stop people from scratching themselves, you name it. Now the restraints are chemical. We don't put people in padded rooms anymore, Detective. Now the padded rooms are in their own minds. This way,"

Her tone had shifted, he noticed, and now she was speaking in a much more confrontational way, almost sounding like she was picking a fight with him. She pointed him down a side hallway.

They walked down the quiet corridor and Reynard noticed nobody else was around. No one walked the hallways of the basement with them. It was dank and mildew-smelling down there, making him think of mold and mushrooms growing in dark places.

"So, you work on E2 but your office is down in the basement," he asked, his heart suddenly beating a bit faster. Something about this whole thing felt off.

"Yes, just a temporary one. They're fixing up my old office - water leak." She opened a door for him finally at the end of the long corridor and he looked inside to see an ordinary office. He

Escape from the Asylum / Jordan Grupe

went inside and sat down, still anxious and looking around nervously.

"Water," she asked, offering him a bottle from her mini fridge which he took gratefully.

He took a long sip from it and she did the same from her bottle.

"So, what was it you called me over here to say?"

She shuffled through some papers on her desk, as if looking for something.

"Just a second, it's here somewhere. I know it is."

The sound of papers being moved around became distant and faded as his vision started going a bit dark around the edges. He realized his mouth was open and drool was dribbling from the corner of it, warm onto his shirt. The woman was no longer looking through her papers, she was simply staring at him, her eyes studying him.

"Are you okay, Detective," Marcy was asking him in a voice that sounded deflated and drawn out, then deep as if being played in super-slow motion.

He found himself unable to reply. As if in a dream, he watched Marcy's nose begin to drip a steady stream of blood. It poured down into her mouth but she seemed not to notice.

His head turned horrified away from that, the sound of someone entering the room drawing his gaze, and he saw it was Doctor Mertzek. The tall man was dressed in a light tan suit and he had his glasses pulled down low as he stood in the doorway, looking down at him. He stepped into the room uninvited and pulled a tissue from the box on the desk, handing it to Marcy absentmindedly.

"Detective," Mertzek said, his voice a million bees droning and buzzing all at once. "You've come back to see us. How wonderful."

21: The Devil's Advocate

"Why didn't you guys call me sooner?"

"Sorry, Jordan. It's just... You were on leave! You said not to bother you!"

"Unless some fucked-up shit happened - didn't I specifically say to call me if some fucked-up shit happened?"

The two guards looked at the ground dejectedly.

"Yeah," they said together in unison.

"What exactly did the detective say after he came up from the sub basement? Was it *her*? Did he see *her* down there?"

"No, I don't think so. It was that doctor - Mertzek, I think his name is. The whole time he said he was looking for the escaped patient but I could tell the way he talked afterwards that he wasn't actually looking for her down there. He was looking for something else. And what he found, according to him, was the doctor with someone locked in a cage. A woman. And a laboratory full of equipment, some old, some new. I kinda eavesdropped when he called in for backup."

Philip, the supervisor, came into the room. They had been expecting him. But he had a disturbed look on his face.

"Sorry to call you back from paternity leave, Philip, but we needed all the help we could get."

"It's okay," he said. "Leslie's parents agreed to babysit. I've actually got a bit of a personal stake in all of this - I needed to come back."

"What do you mean by that, exactly?"

"My uncle was one of the people killed by that escaped patient."

Escape from the Asylum / Jordan Grupe

"Who's your uncle," Matthew asked, surprised.

"Well, remember I told you guys I had an uncle who's a cop? Well, my Uncle Jim was the detective who got killed. They're not saying anything to the media, but he was the escaped patient's brother in law. My aunt's twin sister, Gertrude, she's the one who's on the run."

"Holy shit. But I still don't understand what this has to do with the sub basement and the doctor running a secret lab down there with human guinea pigs."

"Well, I wasn't sure whether or not I should show you guys this… But here goes. My aunt's twin sister, Gertrude - she was the patient who escaped, right?"

They all nodded.

"I found this note from her in my mailbox the morning of the escape."

He unrolled a letter which had been stuffed in his pocket.

They all read it and gasped one by one at the contents of it.

"Is that true?"

"How is that possible?"

"It's true. And I believe her. Which means she needs our help right now. If I'm right about this, it could change everything."

Faintly, Reynard recognized he was in a hospital. But beyond that he could not tell anything.

People came in and brought him food that he didn't eat, gave him drinks that he didn't touch. Liquid medications that tasted terrible were shot into his mouth and his jaw was held shut, forcing him to swallow them.

After a while, he began to take in his surroundings. This was no ordinary hospital. For one thing, he was in a basement. He could

Escape from the Asylum / Jordan Grupe

tell that this was not right. This was not how things were supposed to be in a hospital. Rats were running past across the damp stone floor beneath the bed, occasionally crawling up on the blankets and sniffing at his face. He knew enough to move when that happened, to do something to frighten them off. If he didn't, they might start to get a taste for him, rather than just looking.

One time a nurse walked in and he managed to get his thoughts together enough to ask her a question that had been lingering on his lips for a while.

"Where am I?"

He realized suddenly that he recognized the woman - it was the woman from the cage who the doctor had been holding prisoner. Now he was in the same position she had been in - albeit the cage was slightly larger.

"You're in the hospital, Detective Reynard. In a very special unit, beneath the asylum. It's Doctor Mertzek's project. You remember him, don't you? He's had his eye on you for a long, long time."

She left the tray of food and drinks on his bedside table and grabbed him by the throat. His hands were tied down and when he tried to stop her he found the ropes cut roughly into his skin. Taking a syringe from her pocket, she squirted some medication into his mouth and then shut it again with a firm grip, like someone giving a pill to a dog.

"Swallow. Swallow it. Good," she said, when he eventually relented. His thoughts soon became a stir-fry once again and he drifted off into a sleep made of terrible dreams.

Time passed quickly for Reynard as he lay in his own soiled clothing, covered in his bodily fluids half the time until the nurse reluctantly came to change him. He felt like a baby again, being broken down from his place as a man and put back into the crib of his infancy. After a while, he didn't even fight her anymore - just let it all happen.

Escape from the Asylum / Jordan Grupe

All day the room was filled with a dull gloom, punctuated only by brief periods of light when the familiar woman would come in to check on him, occasionally with the doctor in tow. Eventually he began to hear the sound of others calling for help from the near distance. Sad, despairing calls for someone to save them from their torment. Other patients of the Mad Doctor, Mertzek.

"Why are you doing this to me?" he asked the nurse one day - he had lost track of how long he had been down there for. It felt like weeks.

"It's all for the greater good, Franklin," she said condescendingly. "You'll see one day. You'll understand when it's all over."

"Understand what? What are you trying to do down here? You're torturing all these poor patients. Why?"

"But you're alone down here, Detective Reynard. There are no other patients in the sub basement but you. The fact that you're hearing those voices means the good doctor's prescription is working. He will be very pleased."

"You're insane. You're all insane."

She smiled as if to say *that's the point.*

Then there was a syringe in his mouth, injecting medication there. His hand reached up to stop her but he was clumsy now. Slow and weak from malnutrition. The only thing in his system was the drugs these people were feeding him. It absorbed faster than he could spit it out, and despite his efforts to stay lucid he was soon drifting again, in and out of consciousness.

"It is time for you to wake up, Detective Reynard." The voice brought him up from his slumber immediately and he found he was in a wheelchair, his arms and legs strapped down tightly. He looked around and saw that he was in a laboratory, a film projector set up beside him. The room was dark and there was a blank white screen in front of him. "It's movie time."

He recognized the voice as Doctor Mertzek, but he was not able to turn far enough around to see him. The film began to play and Reynard saw things he would never be able to forget, as much as he might want to. His eyes were taped open.

"I want you to understand, Detective Reynard, exactly what I plan to do to you. Typically a doctor seeks his patient's consent before doing anything *invasive* but I'm afraid we don't have that luxury. Due to the necessity of this work and a limited pool of research volunteers..."

"You mean innocent sick people you kidnapped against their will," Reynard said with as much disgust and vitriol as he could manage in his current state.

"As I was saying, without these luxuries we have to resort to other means of... recruitment."

"Bullshit, Mertzek. I know what's going on. It took me a while to put it all together, but I figured it out. You knew I was on your trail, that's why you brought me down here. That's why you've been trying to discredit me. I'm not your fucking guinea pig - I'm a squeaky wheel in your machine - and it's not just me, either. I've told other people about what you're doing. Expect somebody to come down here any minute for me, by the way. If you want to get any sort of leniency you should think about what you do next."

"So clever, Detective. Except, I don't think anyone is coming for you. I believe you know a couple things, sure, but not enough to make a case against me. So now I just need to find out what those things are. You can make this so much easier on yourself if you just tell me what you know."

He brought out a small brown vial, which was unlabelled, then stuck a needle into it and began to fill the syringe with clear liquid. Lunging forward without a moment's hesitation, he injected the needle straight into the meat of Reynard's thigh.

The pain was immense, like a nail had been driven into his leg with a hammer. It felt like it had hit the bone with the amount of force that was behind it. Then there was a tingling, itching sensation afterwards. Pain like fire spread from the place where the needle had gone in and Reynard began to feel not only agony, but unease.

It felt like the walls were closing in on him. Like the horrifying man standing over him was growing a hundred feet tall as he grinned at his pain.

"Do you feel it, Detective? Do you feel the burn?"

"Yes," he said.

"What else do you feel, Detective Reynard?"

"I feel... Scared. Scared, and alone."

"Alone because no one is coming for you, isn't that right?"

"I don't know," he said, his voice sounding younger and younger to his ears. Like a five year old who was in trouble now. And that was how he felt as well.

"WHAT DO YOU MEAN YOU DON'T KNOW!?" Mertzek shouted, making him cringe and cower as if the devil himself were screaming at him. At that moment it might as well have been.

"I don't know if Dell believes me or not," he whimpered. "But if he does he might get suspicious and come looking for me. The Lieutenant too."

Mertzek bent over and whispered in his ear.

"You were so close. With everything. I'm going to show you what I've been working on - what you're going to be a part of."

Reynard looked up at him, pain still wracking through his entire body from the injection to his leg.

"What the hell is this? What am I going to be a part of?"

"History," Mertzek said from aloft with his evil grin. "World-altering, life-shattering, *history*."

22: Look Before You Leap

What Doctor Mertzek didn't tell Reynard was about the movie he was going to play for him. Instead, he simply shot him with another needle and hit play on the projector.

The white screen in front of Reynard suddenly showed him various still pictures and videos, all of which made him squirm in his chair and made his mind feel wobbly and weak. He wanted to close his eyes as the images played but he couldn't do so.

He wanted to scream, wanted to run, but was unable to do any of those things. Was only able to watch, horrified, as the video played through the scenes, each more disturbing than the last.

Everything he had ever feared, all of his worst nightmares, they were nothing compared to those images. They made him feel as if the entire world was unreal. As if everything he knew was a lie.

Following the movie was a period of darkness that Reynard preferred not to think about.

The period before the movie he would come to think of as PM - *Pre Movie*. The period afterwards he thought of as AM - *After Movie*. Such was the impact this event had on his life. He would never recover from it, and would be forever altered and flipped upside down as a result of it.

He would try to pretend it didn't happen, but the movie itself was something he would never forget. The images he saw would be burnt into his memory for the remainder of his days, so much so that if he closed his eyes he would see a flash of something from it always. It would be only a frame or a few seconds, but sometimes more than a minute of it would play in his memory banks in the coming days, weeks, and years, and he would black out, becoming unresponsive to those around him. But when he finally came back to himself, at least this time, he came to understand he was no longer underground. He was in a regular hospital room upstairs and his old partner Dell was outside the door, talking to someone insistently in the hallway. "I don't care if he's sleeping right now, they say that's all he does is sleep!"

"Don't raise your voice to me, sir, or I'll have you escorted out of this unit immediately, is that understood," a sharp, stern-sounding woman replied. It wasn't the "nurse" from the basement, though - he would recognize her voice anywhere - and that was a relief.

"I'm *sorry*. It's just... I've been trying for a week to get in here to see him. Can I please just go in and sit with him for ten minutes, to see if he wakes up? I won't disturb him."

She hesitated and Reynard suddenly realized he could speak. He tried to say something and his voice came out in a weak and pitiful croak - completely inaudible.

"I'm afraid that's not possible, sir. It isn't safe. This patient is very ill. I've seen it myself, and..."

"This *patient* is my partner, Detective Franklin Reynard, a policeman who has served this city for decades. He's caught murderers and rapists who would have done it again and again if not for him stopping them. And he's seen a lot of terrible things along the way, things that would change anyone. Regardless of what he's done, he's a good man. A damn fine police detective, and I need to speak with him. Please."

"That's just not-"

"Dell," Reynard finally managed to say in a strangled, hoarse-sounding voice, with a painful effort. "I'm here, Dell."

Then his old partner's face was at the door and he was inside, looking at Reynard with grave concern. He stood over his bed with his eyebrows knit into a frown. "Oh fuck, Reynard... What the hell did they do to you, man?"

"Dell?"

"Yeah it's me."

Escape from the Asylum / Jordan Grupe

He shook his head. It wasn't important now. What was important was getting out of this place. "Dell, they did something to me. Down in the sub basement. You have to believe me, Dell. Whatever they're saying I did, I didn't do any of it. It's all a lie."

His old partner shook his head sadly.

"You punched that guy in the face. One of the nurses who works here. He's still recovering."

"What? No, I don't... I don't remember doing that, Dell. They've been feeding me medication with a syringe in my mouth, injecting it in my leg... "

He lowered his voice conspiratorially.

"I think they put a fucking chip in my head, Dell. I know how that sounds, okay? But, listen to me. I felt it! I can still feel it in there, moving around in my brain like a fucking inchworm! Crawling and poking where it doesn't belong, Dell! You have to believe me, Dell! This isn't me! Just like Gertrude. Oh, God! Gertrude! What day is it!? How long have I been in this place!?"

A nurse was suddenly at the door looking in at them and he realized he'd been speaking quite loudly and rambling as well.

He took a deep breath and tried to look and sound as sane as he possibly could. He understood how this looked.

"Um, yeah, so that's what I've been up to. How about you, how's the family?"

He tried to smile and failed terribly, but to his surprise at least the nurse walked away.

"Fuck, Reynard, what am I gonna do with you?"

"Believe me? Please, Dell. You have to get me the fuck out of here. They're gonna kill me if you don't. Right after they're done with their experiments they're gonna fucking kill me, Dell."

"Why the hell did you have to punch that nurse, Reynard? They have it on tape. If you hadn't done that I could have gotten you

Escape from the Asylum / Jordan Grupe

out of here. But it's on video. You're lucky they're not pressing criminal charges - but it doesn't bode well for your release."

I didn't do it, Reynard wanted to say. But who knew what things he had done while unconscious.

"Reynard? Reynard? Are you there?"

Dell was snapping his fingers in his face and he startled awake from his daydream.

"Oh," he said, feeling dopey and disoriented. "Dell, sorry, what were we talking about?"

"You've been out for five minutes, Reynard... You really don't remember what we were talking about? About the video? You punched a guy in the face and he's in the hospital. Remember?"

"I wish I did, Dell. I wish I remembered a lot of things right now. But I can only think of one damn thing and it's the movie they showed me. It never leaves my brain. The images, they play over and over and over again. Dell, I can't live like this. You have to help me. You have to make it stop!"

The nurse came in again suddenly, looking concerned. She had been eavesdropping outside the door by the looks of things.

"Okay, Officer, it's time for you to go now. We can hear him shouting from down the hall. You're upsetting him. Now, if you'd like to come back I'm going to ask you to wait for a few days. We can't have his progress delayed by emotional visits every day. You understand."

Dell rose to his feet reluctantly, shaking his head.

"I wait this long to come in to see him and you let me stay ten minutes - then tell me I'll have to wait a few days to come back? What about patients' rights?"

"If you wish to come back in two days, call ahead and we'll try to fit your visit in our schedule. That's the best I can do, I'm afraid."

Dell finally relented, said goodbye and left the room. The whole thing felt like it was happening in a dream, and after his old partner had left he wondered sincerely if it had been.

Over the next two days he would alternate between theories, but it was the only thing his mind could fixate on, besides the horrors of the movie screen, which played constantly in his mind.

In one version, he was dreaming it all and no one came to see him. He found this to be the most likely scenario, the more he thought about it. In another, his dead partner, Jim, had come to see him in the night. He awoke to find him standing over his bed, grave dirt in his hair, falling off in clumps when he moved his head, and his face turning pruney from the moisture beneath the ground, macerated and white with decay. Worms crawled out from puckered holes in his cheeks, and from the gaping space where one of his eyes had been. "Talk to the security guard, Reynard," Jim said in those dreams, his voice gravely and hoarse. Then he would stare at him with those dead, empty eyes.

Finally, though, Dell returned. He brought a cup of coffee for Reynard and by the sounds of it he had also brought something for the nurses - a platter of chocolates from a local shop.

"Thank you so much again for the gift, Billy. That was really kind of you. Here, let's see if he's awake. He's been sleeping too much lately anyways," the unfamiliar voice was saying, getting louder as they drew near, their footsteps growing in volume also.

"Wakey, wakey, Franklin! You have a guest. It's your brother! Mr... Quaid, was it?"

"Yes, but call me Billy. Hi, Franklin. How are you doing, buddy?"

"I'm doing fine," he said back, trying to ignore Dell's absurd disguise - a fake beard and dark glasses.

"Great," Dell said, forcing an amiable smile. He turned to look at the nurse. "Oh, I brought him a coffee, is that okay?"

"Of course," she said. "Next time, bring a decaf instead, okay?"

Escape from the Asylum / Jordan Grupe

"I'm way ahead of you," he said, tapping the lid and showing her the chalk pen writing on top, which indicated it as such.

"Perfect," the nurse said with a smile. "Sorry about the trouble getting you in here - he had a visitor from work the other day who just caused nothing but issues. I read the whole report. I'm sure he's very happy just to have his big brother in to see him, though."

Dell smiled and nodded and Reynard tried not to giggle at the idea of him being his brother - they looked absolutely nothing alike. At least this nurse seemed more willing to allow him a guest. Apparently the other one had blackballed Dell so that he couldn't come back. Whatever story she had made up had been serious enough to get him banned completely.

Finally the nurse left and he was left alone with Dell. He took the cup of coffee in his hands and sipped it slowly.

"There's something going on in this hospital, Reynard. I think you were right about Mertzek. The way they went after me after my last visit - they're hiding something. They have to be."

Reynard breathed a sigh of relief. It felt so good to be not so completely alone in his knowledge of what was happening. The adrenaline rush of knowing Dell believed him made him suddenly feel normal again. "Did you find her? Did you find Gertrude?"

"No. She's still on the run."

"You've gotta check her fingerprints. There has to be a record somewhere. That'll prove once and for all whether I'm right. You have to check for me Dell."

"I'm gonna try."

"Please get me out of here, Dell. The tall security guard, he'll know what to do. Jim told me. Somehow he came to me in a dream and told me. It was him. I don't know how I know but I know.. You've gotta find him, Dell. He'll know what to do…"

And with that, Reynard fell asleep again. No matter how hard Dell tried, he would not wake back up.

23: Good Things Come to Those Who Wait

The next day when he awoke, there was a security guard stationed outside his room. He was pretty tall, about six and a half feet, and Reynard wondered if he was the one Jim had told him to find in his dream.

That idea, the thought that something communicated to him from a dead man in a dream could be real, would not have seemed rational to him before, but he was finding suddenly he believed in many more things than he once had.

The reason for this was simple - Jim was not the only dead person he had seen recently. Since his time in the basement he had seen more than one. Ghosts would pass through his room sometimes, waking him up from his sleep. It was only at certain times of the night - between three and four AM, he noticed. They appeared to be former patients, and some were raving and angry, others pleasant and docile. But none seemed aware of him or of each other. All of them were semi-transparent and looked pale blue in colour as they went about their idle business.

He dared not mention these things to anyone, not even Dell. He couldn't help but wonder if it was a product of his mind being constantly asleep, as if he were dreaming while awake.

"Good morning," said the guard, standing up from his chair.

He came into the room and looked at Reynard with pity. "You really did a number on yourself last night. How are you feeling?"

Reynard realized suddenly that his forehead hurt very badly. Not like your typical headache, though. This felt different.

"What happened? I don't remember anything after... after my brother left."

"Ha, your brother. Yeah, right. Well, your *brother* didn't tell me you were in this bad shape. You really don't remember, huh? Banging your head against the wall over and over again?"

"No, nothing. I haven't exactly been myself lately. Unfortunately it sounds like it's entirely possible judging by how my head feels today. You talked to him, then? He told you the situation?"

The security guard took a step back and looked around outside the room. Then he came back in.

"Listen, I've seen some shit in this place, okay? If there's anybody who's gonna believe you, it's me. But I need to hear it from you. Straight from the horse's mouth. We need to have an understanding between us that we're on the same page. I don't know how you found out about me, or who told you to contact me, but you did the right thing. I'm probably the only person on the damn planet who can actually help you right now, but you need to tell me the truth. Now, what exactly did you see in the sub basement?"

Reynard hesitated, unsure if he should trust this complete stranger who seemed to know far more than anyone else he had spoken to. He decided it was worth a chance.

"I saw Doctor Mertzek, experimenting on somebody. She ended up working for him down there, as his nurse. Maybe he brainwashed her somehow. He kept me down there too, for I don't even know how long... When I woke up I was here, in this ward, and they told me I hit someone, that I'm committed here against my will now. But I don't remember any of that part - just being locked up in that cell in the basement. And the rats. I remember the rats, too."

"And you're sure? You saw all of this in the sub basement for yourself?"

"Not only did I see it, I lived it! I was down there, a fucking prisoner! He had people in cages! There's probably still more of them down there!"

Escape from the Asylum / Jordan Grupe

The security guard put his finger to his lips.

"Shh, they'll hear you. The nurses here think I'm keeping an eye on the floor right now while they're doing their morning briefing, so we've got maybe ten minutes - fifteen tops. Your whole story about your partner being your brother is done, by the way. They figured it out and he's not allowed back in here. They don't take kindly to being lied to."

"Shit. How the hell can they do that? Is it normal for them to restrict visitors like this?"

"They can if they feel like it's hindering your progress. But usually no, they don't do things like this. I get the feeling someone is taking a very special interest in you here - probably another doctor who's friends with Mertzek. Maybe they're in on this whole thing, maybe they're just helping him out. But either way, they're watching you very closely."

"So you believe me? Please, tell me that you at least believe me."

"I believe you. Trust me, I've seen things here that make what you're talking about sound like a day at the beach. Things I don't even tell my own family, things I'll take with me to my grave. People would lock me up in here if I told them what I've seen."

Reynard was genuinely curious. "Like what?"

The guard hesitated, looking out the door again. Then he took his hands out from his pockets and spread them out in front of him as if offering up himself to Reynard. In a way, he was.

"I don't have time for all of it right now, but I'll give you something. So maybe you'll know I'm on your side. You've seen that old mansion out back, right? Century Manor?"

"Sure, everybody in town knows that place."

"Right," the guard said. "But I'm one of the only people who remembers it burning down."

Escape from the Asylum / Jordan Grupe

Reynard thought long and hard about that. He had lived in this town his whole life, and he knew the history here. That building had stood for a century and a half, hence its name.

"Century Manor... It never burnt down, kid. I don't know what to tell you."

"It did, though. But then one day it was just miraculously back standing again, unscathed as if that had never happened. As if the fire, the insidious plot we managed to stop, as if none of that had ever happened."

After all Reynard had seen, he couldn't argue with the guy. Strange things were certainly happening in this place, and he had seen bits and pieces of it.

"Alright, I'll buy it. What does that have to do with what's happening now?"

The guard thought about that for a few moments.

"I think it's all connected. Just like the tunnels, everything in this place is connected. That sub basement, I don't know how to explain it, but there's a lot of history down there. I've seen some of it, but not the parts you've seen. When I went down there the last time, I stumbled across something I can't explain. It wasn't just me, either. I've got other people who can vouch for me. There's a power running through this place. Samantha - she called them ley lines."

"Who the hell is this Samantha? Can she help us?"

"No, we wouldn't want the sort of help she would offer. For all I know, she could be behind all of this."

"So, *who is she?*"

The guard sighed, looking at him with an expression like distrust, as if unsure whether he'd believe what he said next. "Nowadays, she's a ghost. But around here, that doesn't count for much."

Reynard had a million other questions but the guard stopped him.

"Listen, time is of the essence. I can get you out of here, right now. But you have to do what I say - exactly how I say it. No questions asked, got it?"

"Okay," Reynard said, nodding. He was feeling awake and lucid for the first time in a while. The rush of adrenaline was pumping through his veins and it felt good to have a chance, finally, to get out of this place.

"What size shoes are you?"

"Twelve," Reynard told him. "Why do you ask?"

"That'll be close enough. I need you to hit me."

"No, man I can't do that!"

"You have to, it's the only way. It doesn't have to be hard, it's just for the cameras. But it's gotta connect and it's gotta look real. Then take my jacket, my hat, my shoes, and my badge. You're gonna go up to the door leading out of here with your head down low, the hat covering your face. The ID badge is gonna be clipped to your pocket just like I have it here, okay?"

Reynard couldn't believe he was nodding and saying, "Okay," but he was. He couldn't help it. He needed to get out.

"The guard in the booth out there won't stop you. He's new so he'll think you're another guard. Just keep your head down and go straight out through the door that leads to the elevator. Tell him on the intercom to send the elevator down to level one and go out the door to your right. That will lead you to the parking lot and from there you're a free man. Dell said he'll be waiting in the neighborhood across the street in a white car. You got all that?"

Reynard nodded his head and agreed he would try.

"Alright, Detective. Then do it. Give me your best shot," the security guard said, holding his chin out. "It's gotta be the face. You have to make it look like you knocked me out. I'll play it that way a few minutes - long as I can - to buy you some time."

Escape from the Asylum / Jordan Grupe

Reynard took a few deep breaths and then against all of his instincts he did it. He punched the poor stranger in the face with a right hook. The security guard fell down like a sack of potatoes and Reynard immediately felt extremely guilty and wondered if he was okay, but he didn't have time to ask.

He put on the hat, shoes, and bright yellow jacket, feeling exposed as soon as he had it on. The ID badge was still pinned to the front. After a brief look down at the guard on the floor, he walked out of the room and strode up the hall, trying to look as official as he could. Despite the guard's stolen shoes, his pants were the cheap blue hospital ones with a flimsy drawstring and no fly. He felt like a foolish imposter walking quickly down the hall like that, thinking any second someone would stop him and it'd all be over.

Halfway to the door, about fifty feet into his escape, his eyelids began to droop. He started to suddenly feel very, very tired. All the adrenaline in him was fighting against whatever force was opposing it, but was outmatched. His legs started to feel heavy and clumsy, his vision becoming like a movie with missing frames whenever he turned his head.

Regardless, he made his way to the door. It now looked very far away. Fighting through the medication, he lumbered forward and finally made his way to the exit and looked up at the camera.

Another patient was standing there, eyeing him suspiciously.

The door clicked open and Reynard went out, shutting the door quickly behind him. The Mag-lock snapped back into place and immediately the other patient was at the glass door, looking through it at him. The window fogged up with his breath as he stared and raised a finger to point at him, his hair sticking up in random directions from bed-head.

"You're not staff. He's not staff," the man's voice began to say through the door, the sound of him muffled but still audible.

Reynard turned and began to quickly walk to the next door. It clicked open and he heard the voice of the patient behind him still

Escape from the Asylum / Jordan Grupe

protesting, but gradually fading away. He went through the next door and into an alcove security checkpoint. Keeping his head down, he walked to the next door and waited for the click of it opening. Nothing happened.

He didn't want to look up at the security guard stationed in the booth to his left, the one controlling access to the unit and to the doors he was trying to go through. He was too scared and worried of being caught. Preferring to be rude than to be noticed, he kept looking straight ahead.

Finally, the door clicked open ahead of him and he turned the handle and went through. He was almost in the clear now, it was just a matter of going down the elevator and then leaving through the exit door on the main floor.

Pressing the button for the elevator, he waited for it, tapping his foot impatiently as sweat poured down the sides of his face. Any second, he knew, staff members on the floor would respond to the yelling patient and chase after him. It was only a matter of time.

DING!

The elevator door opened and he got inside quickly, keeping his head down, knowing there were still cameras everywhere. He felt exposed inside the steel cage and went to quickly hit the button for the main floor. But there were no buttons. His fogged mind tried desperately to remember what he was supposed to do.

"Uhh, what floor," an impatient voice asked over the intercom.

"Ground," he said back, unsure if that was right. He could no longer remember what he was supposed to do. Only that he needed to get out of this place. He felt like a swimmer coming up to the surface for air, so close yet still so far away from that gasping breath and feeling as if he could die if he didn't get it at this instant. He was so close. After several long moments of shaky descent, the elevator stopped and a sound of the door rattling open could be heard, but the one in front of him was still closed.

Escape from the Asylum / Jordan Grupe

Momentarily confused and disoriented, it took him several moments to realize that the door behind him was now closing. It was an elevator that let you on in the front and let you off in the back. He had been on this elevator before and yet he had forgotten that. Such was his mental state at that moment. He stuck his arm in the gap quickly and it opened up for him once more.

He felt suddenly dizzy and extremely exhausted. Trying to move his leg forward, at first it wouldn't budge. He raised it woodenly and was surprised when the door began to close on him again.

The drugs were affecting him - whatever they were feeding him it was strong, and seemed to come and go in waves at the most inopportune times. He lunged forward and wedged his arm into the door gap just as it was closing, prying it open and stumbling triumphantly from the box, feeling as if he had just won a fight with a machine bent on his destruction. Turning back to look at it, the thing seemed to be laughing at him with vaguely human features. He shook his head and tried to clear these spiralling thoughts laced with hallucinations.

To his right, the door to the outside world stood - like a golden gate to paradise - the light beaming in from outside. He slammed into it and pushed down hard on the handle. It wouldn't budge.

Reynard's heart was hammering fast in his chest. This was it. They had caught him. Someone had called the security booth and at the very last second they had locked the door. He felt as if he could cry.

Then the speaker mounted on the wall to his left crackled to life and he heard a garbled voice say, "Sorry about that," and the door's lock clicked open.

"No problem," Reynard heard himself say, and pushed down on the door handle, stumbling out into the fresh air of the parking lot.

For a moment, all he could do was stand there and breathe it in, deeply into his lungs, savouring it. He let out his breath and heard the sounds of sirens in the distance, and ran.

24: Hit The Nail on The Head

"Reynard, thank God, you made it," Dell said as he scrambled into the car.

The run through the parking lot had left him bruised and aching from slamming into vehicles accidentally and he had heard the voices of people chasing after him by the end of it, yelling at him to come back.

"Drive, quick, we gotta get outta here," he managed to say through slurred lips.

"Are you alright? What the hell have they been feeding you today," Dell asked, pulling away from the curb and speeding off.

"I don't have the slightest..."

Reynard didn't remember anything after that, as his aching, weary mind finally succumbed to the drugs pumping through his bloodstream and he fell fast asleep.

When he awoke, Reynard found that he had no idea where he was.

The room around him was bare and empty and he was alone in it. There was a chair in one corner and a bed in which he was currently laying. That was about it, aside from a door and a light above him on the ceiling, which had been turned off so he could sleep.

As if I needed more sleep, he thought to himself bitterly. And yet he felt as if he did. He felt as if he could sleep more right now, and stay dreaming for a million, billion years.

What's wrong with me?

Dell entered and appeared surprised to see him awake.

"Hey, how are you feeling? You really sleep like the dead when you're out, y'know that?"

"I never used to. I was always a light sleeper. The slightest noise would get me up at night."

"Huh, well, whatever they were feeding you should be out of your system by now. At least I'd hope. But I'm no doctor."

"That's a good thing as far as I'm concerned, Dell," Reynard said. "After what I've been through, I don't think I'll trust a doctor again in my life."

He was rubbing his head, his eyes still bleary and his mind foggy.

"So, catch me up. What did I miss?"

Dell sat down in the chair and looked at him solemnly.

"You missed a helluva lot, that's what. Allison is gone from the hotel where she was under police protection, meaning we don't know where she's gotten off to. And meanwhile Gertrude - who we think might be Allison, but we'll call her Gertrude for simplicity sake - is still missing."

"So we're in even worse shape than we were before. Do you have any good news for me, Dell?"

His partner actually revealed a tiny smirk and he said, "I'll let the guest of honor explain that. Ah, here he is now."

The tall brown-haired security guard who had broken him out of the asylum entered the room, sporting a still-pink shiner which had been given to him courtesy of Reynard himself.

"You got a hell of an overhand right, Detective, I'll give you that," he said, giving a smile which said he was feeling okay despite his soon-to-be black eye. It was starting to swell shut and he appeared to be having difficulty seeing from it. "I did say it didn't have to be a *hard* punch, or did I forget that part?"

"Shit. Sorry about that," said Reynard, standing up, going over to the man to apologize sincerely. "Are you okay?"

"Just bustin' your balls, man," the guard laughed, and Dell broke out in a smile too. "I couldn't help it! It's all good - I used to get my ass kicked worse than that back in Catholic middle school."

"Oh, good. I'm glad you're alright. Honestly I didn't think it would give you a black eye. Maybe I'm stronger than I thought."

"Yeah, you're a regular Floyd Mayweather. You might have picked the wrong profession."

"Can you fill me in from your end of things? Dell says you've got something that might help. By the way, before we get to that, what's your name? We never properly introduced ourselves, did we?"

"No, I guess we didn't."

He stuck out his hand to shake and Reynard took it in a firm grip, pumping up and down twice as his father had taught him to do so many years ago.

You can tell a lot about a man by his handshake, he remembered him saying - and it had proven true over the years. Some men gripped your hand so hard that you couldn't even squeeze theirs back, as if your hand was being strangled by theirs. Others gave a limp fish grip and that was almost worse. But the security guard gave a firm, simple handshake and it made him feel that much more as if he could trust him.

"My name's Jordan. It's a pleasure to meet you, Detective Reynard. Although not under these circumstances, of course."

Reynard couldn't help it, he brought the man in for a bear-hug, overcome with sudden unexpected emotions.

"Thank you for getting me out of there. I owe you. I owe you big time."

"Hey, happy I could help you out. Dell told me about all you've done for this city - it was the least I could do."

Escape from the Asylum / Jordan Grupe

Reynard wiped tears out of his eyes and felt his lip trembling as he spoke, still feeling as if he could crumble to the floor at any second after all that had happened. It was strange, one moment he felt like himself, and then the next it was like he was breaking down, as if his brain was malfunctioning and releasing hormones with intentional ill-timing. But he guessed that was just the lingering effects of the polypharmaceutical plethora of drugs he had been given.

"What can you tell us about our current situation? It sounds like you know that place better than anyone. Do you know what Mertzek is up to?"

The guard looked deep in thought.

"This situation is a little different than the one we experienced before. That hospital... Well, there's some powers at work in that place that are strong enough to influence others, and I'm beginning to suspect even to completely control others."

"These powers, you said, brought a building back from the ashes. Century Manor - which you told me had burned down. If they can do something like that, I'm sure an old school possession like in 'The Exorcist' wouldn't be out of the question. But who is this ghost controlling," Reynard asked, and Dell raised his eyebrows. "Sorry, Dell, I see that look on your face, but I've seen them. I can't explain it, but I've seen them in that place. Ghosts are real - I've no doubts about that."

"Detective Dell, I can tell you're not a believer. And trust me, I wasn't either until what happened to me. It changed my outlook on a lot of things," the guard said.

"What exactly happened," Dell asked. "Hey, after everything we've been going through, I'm willing to keep an open mind."

"It's a long story. Maybe one day I can tell you the whole thing, but for right now I'll give you the jist of it."

The guard took a deep breath before continuing.

"It all started with a voice calling for help from behind a closed door in the west end of the basement. A little girl trapped in an abandoned room. At least, that was what I thought at the time..."

The three men sat around the room silently after the guard finished his story. Despite his efforts at condensing it, the tale was a long one. Even after everything Reynard had seen, it took him a while to process it.

Secret tunnels leading to an underground cavern, a cult of escaped mental patients living beneath the asylum in a cavernous village. Ley lines, mind control, and cannibalism? Oh my.

"Alright, I'll take you at your word," he said. "I can't pretend the things I've seen aren't just as impossible. And I've been reading liars my whole career - you're either an impeccably good one, or you're telling us the truth."

Dell seemed less easily convinced. A few times during the guard's story he had appeared visibly distressed, as if wondering whether he had chosen the right side in all this. Reynard had to remind himself that Dell had not seen everything he had witnessed. He was taking all of this on faith from two men who he barely knew. And that was a lot to take on faith.

When he spoke up, Reynard was surprised to hear him voice his agreement also.

"I wasn't sure if I believed you, until Reynard said that just now. But he's right. You're not a liar. You might be completely insane, but you're not a liar."

Dell looked around at both of them to see they were staring at him with their jaws hanging down.

"What? Like I said, you're either telling the truth or it's just the truth in your deranged mind. But I'll choose to believe it's the former over the latter for the time being."

Reynard looked at the security guard and tried to decide what their next move should be.

"So, are these three isolated events related? The ghost girl, the mad scientist Mertzek, and the missing patient? That's the real question. We have to know what we're dealing with to stop it."

"I still think Samantha's ghost has something to do with all this, especially after all that's happened - Century Manor's rise from the ashes, the similarities of Mertzek's fascination with the abandoned sub basement... Not to mention the fact that he's kidnapping patients under the auspices of them going missing. There's too many similarities not to ignore. I don't know if she's possessed him or if she's influencing him somehow, but this has her fingerprints all over it. But to get to the bottom of all that we need to catch Mertzek and the *real* Gertrude. I have a feeling one will come after the other like dominoes falling."

Dell spoke up for the first time in a while.

"We need to find out where that bastard Mertzek is operating now - we find his new lab, we find him, and we find the proof. Then we can finally take him down."

25: It Takes One to Know One

With a plan now firmly in their minds, the three of them set about investigating where exactly Mertzek's new secret lab would be located.

The lab had to be accessible from the sub basement, for him to have access to the tunnels that were so vital to his operation. Not to mention his power-source was located down there - the energy he was tapping into for his mysterious endeavours.

Reynard was wanted and reported missing, while Dell and Jordan had managed to avoid any suspicion during the escape. Still, they didn't feel comfortable leaving Reynard alone by himself, considering how he had been feeling. Instead, Jordan went back to the hospital to see what information he could find out while Dell stayed with him at the safehouse.

The two of them sat around trying to figure out how exactly they were going to outsmart Mertzek, who seemed to be two steps ahead of them at all times.

Reynard couldn't help it, as he sat there in a chair in the living room he replayed his captivity in the sub basement over and over again in his mind, thinking about the time he was trapped down there, rats crawling all over him, sniffing at his face. He thought about the movie they had forced him to watch which had warped his mind so he could no longer trust his own brain. And he thought about the words spoken to him by the nurse who was not a nurse while he was underground.

It's all for the greater good. You'll see one day. You'll understand when it's all over.

Reynard kept thinking about those words over and over in his head, getting angrier and angrier. *How dare they presume to know what was best for him, to make such a decision for him as to take over his mind for their own purposes? What exactly was it that they had done to him? What experiment had he been the unwitting subject of? And would he become subjugated by the doctor as she had been? A disciple of his mad doctrine?*

The woman had said something else to him, too. When he had complained that he was being tortured, that it was inhumane what they were doing to the patients they had taken.

The subject can never know the variables, otherwise it negates the objective of the experiment. But I promise you, if you knew what we are doing, what he has planned, you would gladly give yourself up to be a part of this. It'll change the world completely.

She had sounded mad, and he had said so. But it hadn't changed what they had done to him.

What did they do to you, Reynard? Why does the back of your neck itch ever so slightly, as if an insect were living back there, beneath the skin? And why can you see glimpses of dead things? Things with worms crawling from their faces and empty eye sockets as they roam the earth in a never-ending purgatory of an afterlife inside that prison of a hospital???

He thought again about the itch on the back of his neck. Reaching with his hand, he felt around for the spot where he always wanted to scratch. The spot where he had dreamt that Mertzek had implanted something, while he was sleeping. That dream had been so long ago, it seemed to be almost in another life.

"Dell, this is gonna sound crazy, but can you get a mirror?"

"There's one in the bathroom," he replied.

"Okay, great. But I need another one. Is there a hand mirror somewhere? A shaving mirror? Something like that?"

Dell went into another room and came back with a hand mirror.

"What's this about," he asked, handing it to Reynard.

"Follow me."

They both went into the bathroom and Reynard held the mirror up behind his head, looking into the reflection of the other mirror above the sink and examining the back of his neck with it, like a barber showing off the back of a haircut.

"FUCK. Just what I was afraid of."

"What," Dell asked.

Reynard felt the lump with his fingers, examining it as closely as he could in the mirror. He thought about it for a while before asking.

"Do you have a razor blade and a bottle of alcohol?"

"Okay, now I'm starting to get concerned. What do you need those for?"

Reynard pointed at the base of his skull, at the back of his head, lifting up his thinning hair.

"See that scar?"

Dell looked for a few long moments before saying that he did.

"Looks fresh, right?"

"Yeah. How'd you get that?"

Reynard turned around again and looked him dead in the eyes, determination set in his mind at what he planned to do.

"Listen, I think they implanted some sort of device in the back of my neck. Something that releases medication. I've been noticing the effects for a while but didn't know how it was still happening out here. With this thing, Mertzek can make me sleepy, he can make me see things, can make me seem like I'm losing my mind. Mertzek wanted to discredit me and stop any chance of being arrested. But what if he put in something else too? A failsafe like a cyanide capsule in case I get too close? I need to get it out."

Dell looked at him, shaking his head with a concerned expression on his face.

"Reynard, I believe you, okay? Mertzek is capable of something like that, I have no doubt. I know you think I don't trust you a hundred percent because I don't know you as well as Jim did, but I asked around about you Reynard. I talked to people in Homicide, and all of the departments. You're a good person. I know that the things you did aren't really you."

Reynard eyed him uncertainly.

"Why are you saying all this, Dell?"

"Because I can't let you do that. I can't let you try to cut something out of your neck, that close to your spine, when we don't even know what it's attached to or how big it is or anything! What if you remove it and you die? Did you think of that? What if it's attached to your spinal cord or to some nerve or artery or something and you become paralyzed or bleed out? We need to get you to a doctor to deal with whatever that is - but you can't just cut it out yourself!"

He thought about this for a while, debating what to say to convince Dell he was right, but the more he debated the more he began to realize that he didn't know what would happen, and that Dell was playing it safe. If he just tore it out, who knew what might happen?

"Shit, you're right. I can't believe I'm saying this, but you're right, Dell."

"Sorry, Reynard. I wish I wasn't."

"So what the hell am I supposed to do? Just walk around with this damn thing implanted in my neck, not knowing what it is or when it's gonna be set off? I could be in the middle of a firefight and suddenly I need to take a nap, or worse yet start tripping like I took a sheet of acid. Been there, too."

Dell put a hand on his shoulder and looked at him reassuringly.

"Hey, listen. At least this time you'll have backup."

Escape from the Asylum / Jordan Grupe

After a couple days of planning and reconnaissance work from multiple security guards, as well as the help of a hacker friend whose identity was unknown to Reynard, they eventually located the place where Mertzek was conducting his ongoing research.

Philip, another guard who worked with Jordan, managed to follow the doctor back to a commercial district in the east end of town, where rents were cheap and many buildings were abandoned and empty. With a simple check from Dell using the police database, they managed to find out that he was indeed paying to rent the property, although he was using an alias.

The building was a large warehouse structure with very few windows and plenty of cameras.

"He'll have an escape all planned out," Reynard said as they sat around discussing what they were going to do. "We have to account for that. A vehicle will be hidden somewhere, maybe two of them. He's always three steps ahead of us, this time will be no exception. We need to find out exactly how he's going to counteract us and plan ahead for it."

Philip, Jordan, and Dell were sitting around the living room and the coffee table was littered with photos and written ideas. "Allison" was still missing from the hotel where she had been under police surveillance and they believed if they were right about her true identity, she was hiding out with Mertzek - likely inside the building he had been visiting. He had been photographed bringing groceries, water, and other supplies to the place, in far greater quantities than what he needed for himself.

"The two of them are there, I have no doubt," said Reynard. "He's probably got others too, not of their own free will. Just like down in the sub basement, he's continuing his experiments... *For the greater good,* as his assistant liked to say."

"Darlene Walbeck," Dell said, producing a photograph. "Is this her? She was a patient of Mertzek's up until four weeks ago when she absconded from the hospital. After an extensive search we have yet to locate her anywhere, despite her past tendencies to seek out close family and friends when unable to find a living situation. We believe she may also be working in Mertzek's pop-up laboratory in this warehouse building."

Reynard nodded.

"That's her. I'll never forget that woman's face. Not after what they did to me," he said, rubbing his neck where the scar was. When this was all over he would have to go see a very good surgeon - and it would be a miracle if they believed his story.

"Okay, so it sounds like it's three on five. We just need to cut off all of his escape routes," Philip said.

"Five? Who's the other person? I only count four of us," said Reynard, looking around the room. He counted Philip and Jordan - the two security guards, and Dell and himself.

"You're right, I miscounted," Phillip said, smiling. He was looking at his phone with a mischievous grin on his face. "There's gonna be six of us now."

Suddenly there was a knock at the door and Jordan got up to answer it.

"I guess Dell never told you."

"Hey, I didn't want to spoil the surprise. It was your big secret."

Reynard looked back and forth between the two men, trying to figure out what the hell was going on.

"Tell him already, he looks like he's going to explode," Dell said.

But just as Philip opened his mouth to do so, the door opened and a woman and a small child stepped inside. The boy looked scared and nervous, the woman slightly less so.

On the forehead of the familiar-looking woman was a slightly-fading blue tattoo, reading one word:

BETRAYED

26: Ignorance is Bliss

"Detective Reynard, I'd like to introduce you to my aunt, Allison. I'm sorry for keeping this from you, I really am. But I had to know you believed her before I could tell you the truth."

He couldn't understand how she was standing right there in front of him with her kid. The end of this terrible ordeal for the first time felt within sight for Reynard and he nearly leapt with joy at the sight of them.

Reynard began to laugh, first just a giggle, then a chuckle, then he was doing a full belly-laugh, much to the surprise of the other five people in the room.

"What the hell's so funny, Reynard," Dell asked. "Excuse my language in front of the youngster."

He almost couldn't stop laughing for a while, but eventually he did and answered his partner's question between fits of giggling.

"We looked so hard everywhere for you two, and you just walk in the front door," Reynard giggled, and found he was having trouble shutting it off. He vaguely wondered if it had something to do with the device in his neck that Mertzek had implanted there.

He no longer felt any doubt there was something there, planted just below his skin. Whether there was actually any danger in taking it out remained to be seen, but he was unable to even attempt to remove the thing himself.

"I'm just glad you're safe," he said, finally settling down. "Allison."

The boy looked up at the woman with a look of genuine curiosity and wonderment, as if hearing this for the first time, and Reynard couldn't help but ask.

"You do know that this is your mom, don't you Greg?"

The boy stuttered and mumbled before finally saying something coherent.

"She says she is. But I didn't believe her. After a while, though, I started to wonder if maybe..."

He trailed off, looking as if he still wasn't sure, and Allison appeared hurt by that but only vaguely, as if she had gotten used to the sting of him saying such things.

"She is, Greg. Listen, do you remember me? I was your dad's partner. Do you remember him talking about his partner, Reynard? We met a few times, just for a few seconds."

The boy looked at him, squinting his eyes with inspection, before finally nodding.

"Yeah, I remember."

"Well, I can vouch for her. The lady who you thought was your mom, that's her twin. They switched about a year ago and they took your mom to the hospital in her place, even though she hadn't done anything wrong. The woman who has been claiming to be your mother, that's your aunt Gertrude. I know this is hard to believe, but it's true."

"It's like being in the hospital all over again," Allison said. "I can't convince people I'm sane no matter how hard I try. I never would have known what that felt like before being a patient there. Nobody believes you when you tell them you're not crazy. When I got emotional it counted against me. If I tried to be logical about it, they'd say how *calculating* I was, as if I were a sociopath. But I'm not!"

"I know you're not," said Philip. "We believe you. And you should too, Greg. This really is your mom. I can't imagine how difficult this must be for you but you have to believe what we're telling you is true."

"The last time I spoke to Jim, he told me," said Reynard. "I just didn't believe it or I didn't want to at the time. But now that you're here and I'm looking you in your eyes, it's so obvious. I remember you from when you had my wife and I for dinner. Before she passed away. There's something in your eyes that isn't in hers. Maybe he doesn't remember, but I do. And Jim's words made me realize that. I think he felt really sorry, Allison. There was a lot of remorse in his voice when he said that - like he couldn't believe he hadn't noticed it sooner. We were both shitty husbands - neither one of us paid attention like we should have. I have to know, though, what exactly happened that morning at the house?"

Allison looked up, trying to dry the tears in her eyes.

"I hid in the woods for a while after leaving the hospital. I was too afraid of being spotted in the daytime, walking the streets. After it got dark I went back to the house and hid outside in the bushes, looking in through the windows at my sister, coveting her stolen life with my family. They were all sitting around the television in the living room, laughing and watching some show. I just watched them for a long time, and then waited for them to go to bed, hoping they'd leave a door unlocked. I needed to talk to Jim, to try and explain what happened, but I wasn't sure how he'd react or if he'd call the police the second he saw me.

"Luckily, I think he could tell there was something going on. He knew me so well that he could tell just by looking in my eyes, same as you. He went to bed late and I threw a pebble at the window, like in some cheesy rom-com, and lured him outside to talk to me. After a while he invited me inside, and I could tell he believed me. He picked up the phone and was about to call the police when Gertrude walked in..."

Reynard turned to look at Greg again.

"We're gonna find proof. Greg, just try to keep an open mind, okay? We're gonna prove to you that this is your real mom. That other lady was tricking you and your dad for a long time. But your dad called me on the phone, he told me, okay? He told me to tell you that this is your real mom. He needed you to know that, Greg."

For the first time, a glimmer of something like belief shined in his eyes, and he looked up at the woman he had believed kidnapped him.

What felt like a very long time passed before the boy spoke. But when he did, none of them would have guessed what he said.

"Mom?"

A little while after that they sent Gregory to bed and Allison finished her story. Reynard needed to know what happened after that, but it wasn't fit for the young boy's ears. Allison's eyes dripped tears in a steady stream as she continued.

"Gertrude was always stronger than me. She was always better at defending herself and she beat me up more than once when we disagreed. When she came out into the kitchen holding that knife, I knew there was going to be trouble. Jim... He pushed me out of the way at the last second. She was coming for me, but Jim saved me."

Reynard handed her a tissue, nodding for her to go on.

"She got even madder after that, because she knew. She knew he believed me. So she went after him next and she started stabbing him, over and over and over again while he tried to fight her off. He tried so hard, but eventually she tripped him to the floor and he hit his head. And then she came after me. I thought she was going to kill me but then she just grabbed hold of me and started tying me up. Stuffed a T-shirt in my mouth to keep me quiet. She whispered in my ear and said she was going to make sure I went away again forever. She said it was my fault that things hadn't been normal for her. She liked my life and she didn't want to give it up. She liked being a mother after all, and she wanted to keep Greg for herself."

"Then she got in the car and left. I just had to lay there and watch while Jim bled on the floor. When she got back she said I would never be free again. Jim had other plans, though. He was barely able to move but he was still alive. He'd been working on freeing me from the ropes she'd tied me up with and he stood up and started to fight her again. He was pale as a sheet, still losing blood by the minute, but he grabbed hold of her and told me to get Greg and to run. So that's what I did. I ran into his bedroom and picked him up in my arms like he was a toddler again. I hugged him tight and I ran.

"When I got outside, Jim's car was blocked in by a blue Honda, the keys still in the ignition. Of course, later I'd find out it was that poor security guard's car, who Gertrude had murdered. We took the car and ran, heading up north."

Reynard sat back, taking this all in. Allison continued telling him what had happened after that and soon all of them realized they would not be resting at all that night. There was far too much to do and too much to talk about.

The plan they came up with was not without its faults, Reynard thought to himself as they went over it for the final time that night.

Mertzek was smart and he would expect them to be coming for him. The prospect of all of this being a trap occurred to him and he brought that up, but nobody seemed to believe it. Reynard was the only one who had truly experienced the mad brilliance of the doctor and he did not believe they would fool him so easily.

He was right.

They prepared to leave for the warehouse late that night, around 2AM, choosing to leave Allison and Greg at the safehouse. After giving it plenty of consideration, it seemed smarter to leave them there as a precaution and also as a safeguard against Mertzek. If he managed to outsmart them, at least Allison and Greg would be able to corroborate their story - although they doubted it would do much good. A child and an escaped mental patient were not the most reliable witnesses, after all.

Reynard left the house with Dell, Philip, and Jordan, and they drove to the warehouse district and parked outside the building they had traced Mertzek to.

"According to Philip's surveillance, he's been here every night this week and he tends to stay all night," Dell said when they were outside. "His car is here, so we can be fairly certain he's here too, but on the off-chance this is a trap, we have a contingency plan, at least."

"There's three exits," Philip said to them as they all looked over the photos he had printed showing various angles of the building. "The back two can be covered by one person easily enough. That leaves three of us to go in through the front, then one person remains outside to catch anybody trying to escape. We should have the upper hand no matter what."

"Philip, I nominate you to wait out back. You've got your hunting rifle so at least you've got something to defend yourself," said Jordan. "I'll go in with them through the front. I'll try to help any way I can."

They got out of the car and took their positions, Dell, Jordan and Reynard at the front door, Philip at the back.

With nothing else to lose, Reynard turned the door knob and tried to see if it was unlocked. It wasn't, but they had expected that. He pulled out his lockpick kit and began to work at the door. It took him several minutes, but eventually he managed to finagle it. The tumblers clicked with a small but satisfying sound and the lock turned to the left and was open.

The three men entered the building and found themselves immediately in a small waiting room with a desk. It was empty and there were two doors leading in different directions, one to the left and one to the right.

Dell raised two fingers and pointed towards Reynard and Jordan, then he pointed silently towards the door ahead of them to the right. The two of them began moving in that direction, Reynard's heart pounding in his chest. Adrenaline was flowing through his veins and he felt strong and clear-headed.

But at the same time he knew that any second the device he believed was implanted in his skin could release a dose of mind-altering psychotropic chemicals designed by Mertzek to fuck with him. He wished he had been able to remove the thing, but Dell made a good point about the dangers of such an operation being performed by amateurs.

At the same moment, they opened the two doors. Dell looked inside and saw nothing, motioning for Reynard to proceed to the right. Then an instant later he was gone.

Something about this didn't feel right. They had gone in with three people in order to have an advantage. Now they were already down to two and Dell was by himself. Not to mention Reynard's compromised state. But it was too late now as his partner had already gone off down the other hallway with his gun raised. At least he had backup outside and the security guard was with him.

The two of them proceeded down another hallway and found it to be lined with doors on either side. There appeared to be a small office space in this section of the building. All the doors were locked and the lights were turned off inside the rooms. Feeling uneasy, Reynard continued moving past this section. He knew what he was looking for and this wasn't it.

After proceeding through this area, they ended up at a white door beside a desk. Noise could be heard from behind the door and a light was on indicating that someone was inside.

Escape from the Asylum / Jordan Grupe

Reynard raised his index finger to his lips to ask for silence and the guard nodded his head. Then he listened at the door and slowly turned the knob, entering a huge open warehouse space. There were shelves lined up in rows going up to the ceiling.

To his left, a set of stairs led up to a booth that overlooked the room where perhaps a foreman or a manager would sit to survey the employees working in the warehouse. The light was on in this small office space but Reynard couldn't see anyone inside.

Up ahead, he heard a noise. A sound like a glass being set down against a steel table. Then the clanking of more glass and a cough - it sounded like a man working up ahead. Reynard continued moving forward, looking back to see Jordan was still with him. They went down the aisle between the tall shelves and eventually came to an opening.

In the middle of a large empty space in the center of the warehouse, was Mertzek and his assistant, the woman from the sub basement. He had a workstation setup with beakers and a centrifuge, Bunson burners and all manner of chemical implements. He was pouring a vial of something into a glass container sitting atop a digital scale. It began to bubble and hiss, emitting a cloud of bluish smoke.

With his gun drawn and pointed at the doctor, Reynard called out.

"Hands in the air, Mertzek. It's over. We found Allison and she told us everything."

He turned around with the vial still in his brown-gloved hands. He set it down on the table and raised his arms in submission.

"Very good, Detective. Oh, and where's your partner? He must be around here somewhere..."

The sound of tapping on glass could be heard suddenly from the office looking over the warehouse space. Reynard looked up and saw Dell up there with a gun pointed at his head. Standing behind

Escape from the Asylum / Jordan Grupe

him was Gertrude. Dell stared down at Reynard with a remorseful look, the gun pointed at his temple, rubbing against it abrasively. He mouthed the word, "Sorry," and closed his eyes as if submitting to death.

"Shit," Reynard said. "Y'know, I had a feeling this was a trap."

Mertzek laughed and laughed as if that were the funniest thing in the world.

"There's one thing I have to know, Mertzek. Before you kill us, or whatever it is you're gonna do - can you just tell me why? Why are you doing this?"

He looked at them both and then up at Gertrude, who nodded.

"Alright, Detective. Maybe this will illuminate the issue for you. Make you understand why I've spent the last year of my life, dedicated to this singular purpose. You see, I always scoffed when people spoke of the supernatural. Some staff members even talked openly about St. Daniel's being haunted and I would scold them for it, saying such talk would upset the patients. But then, about a year ago, something happened to me when I was walking to my car late one evening. I heard a voice calling to me for help from that old manor at the back of the asylum grounds..."

Reynard heard a soft gasp from the guard standing behind him.

"Samantha," he muttered quietly. "I knew she was involved in all this somehow."

"I went inside that old building, called Century Manor," the doctor continued. "And when I did the door closed shut behind me by itself, leaving me alone in darkness. I tried to turn around, to run from that place, but the door wouldn't budge. It was padlocked shut from the outside, I would find out later.

"Three nights and two days I spent in that place. In that decaying, dark, old mansion. I went inside on a friday night and was finally found hammering on the windows on monday morning, screaming bloody murder, they told me. But I don't remember that part. I only remember bits and pieces of what happened in between, and what came of that weekend in the home of a ghost. I can hear her now, in the back of my mind. Whispering to me, telling me secrets and giving me gifts of wisdom from other worlds. She's telling me now to say hello to your security guard friend, for instance.

"The veil between worlds is thin in places, Reynard. And I have found recently that the veil is especially fragile in the vicinity of St. Daniel's. The veil has begun to tear, and what was on the other side is now bleeding into our world."

Reynard would have thought such talk was madness not so long ago, but now he believed differently. Mertzek seemed to sense this as he looked at him.

"You've seen them, haven't you? Our time together was cut woefully short, due to the constant complaints and intrusions of your partner. That's why we choose people like you, Reynard. People with no family or friends. Nobody sticks up for them. Unfortunately you found a friend. I never did get to see your breakthrough. But you've seen them since, haven't you? The phantoms from the other side?"

He hesitated but eventually nodded, unable to lie.

"I heard them too. Down in the sub basement. I heard the voices of a hundred prisoners down there, near the end. But it was just me locked up, I realize that now."

Mertzek smiled.

"See? You didn't even need me to tell you that. You could already sense it. You can thank me later for the gift I've bestowed upon you. And for your sneak preview of the things to come for all mankind."

This caught Reynard by surprise.

"What? For all mankind? I don't understand."

Escape from the Asylum / Jordan Grupe

Making a tsk, tsk, tsk sound with his lips, the doctor didn't say. But then Reynard looked around at the crates in the warehouse, stacked up to the ceiling. He saw the size of Mertzek's chemistry set compared to the one in the sub basement, and the much larger centrifuge he had acquired.

"You're gonna poison the whole town, aren't you? What are you planning to do, wreck everyone's brain with your sick chemical concoction?"

"Don't you get it, Reynard? The world can be a better place - we can learn so much from our ancestors, and from the ones in other worlds. We can help everyone see through the veil. And perhaps we can bring others through, from the other side. They can help us."

Reynard lifted up his gun, aiming it again at Mertzek's head.

"You're fucking insane. You're a psychiatrist - you're supposed to help people! This isn't helping anyone. The dead need to stay dead! People will kill themselves just to stop seeing these things! They're not meant to exist in our world."

The doctor looked hurt.

"Well, my dear Detective, you couldn't be more wrong. But I can tell you won't be convinced. And if you're not with us, then I suppose you're against us. It's a shame, really. I thought perhaps with your new eyes you would be able to see the light. But I suppose some people are just destined to live in darkness."

Mertzek held up a black remote control in his hand and turned a dial on it to the right.

Suddenly Reynard began to feel his eyelids closing involuntarily again. He wanted more than anything to sleep in that moment, ten times more so than he had ever felt before when he had experienced these effects.

Escape from the Asylum / Jordan Grupe

"Getting sleepy, Reynard? I'm curious, did you try to take it out yet, Detective? The device. Did you find how it was perfectly wrapped around your brain stem and its pain centers so that you would feel the most delicious, excruciating agony for the remainder of your days if you tried to dislodge it?"

He turned another dial and the colours in the room suddenly became brighter, more vivid, seeming to almost light up and glow like fluorescents. His tiredness became a melancholy trip that felt like he was falling down a whirlpool spiralling downwards into black, starless outer space.

Reynard turned to see the security guard's head was bulging and swelling like a lava lamp behind him and he quickly passed him the gun before things got any worse.

He had the momentary ability for critical thought that allowed him to do so, right before he fell into that whirlpool of sad delusions and gut-wrenching hallucinations.

"Take this," he managed to say. "Shoot the sonofabitch if you have to."

And then he went into another world.

Escape from the Asylum / Jordan Grupe

27: A Taste of Your Own Medicine

Reynard stumbled forward into something that felt squishy and wet. When he looked up, he saw it was a giant wall made of a kaleidoscope of colours. It pulsated with energy and from behind him he heard a commotion of sound like a roadway full of cars.

"Where the fuck am I," he asked, his voice echoing loudly, but nobody answered.

There was no memory of how he had gotten there and his heart pounded with fear as he realized he had finally completely lost his mind, just as his mother had.

And just as he thought that, she was there in front of him. Instead of the kaleidoscope of colours and the wall reaching up into the heavens with no end, there was simply a hospital room. Windowless and sad, painted in urine-yellow semi-gloss. The room was full of people who acted like he wasn't there, and spoke about his mother as if she wasn't either. Her face was pale and sad, tears standing in her sleep-hollow eyes as she laid in bed, looking at him. The white-coated men with glasses and no eyes behind the reflections stood around watching them impassively, taking notes.

"You turned out just like I did," she told him. "Just like I knew you would. You'll spend the rest of your life here, son. You never stood a chance."

And then suddenly it was him laying in the hospital bed, with doctors all around, staring at him with clipboards in their hands. One of them looked familiar, he realized, and he studied his face carefully.

It looked like Mertzek, only younger.

Escape from the Asylum / Jordan Grupe

There was a feeling in the back of his neck like an itch and he scratched it absentmindedly. The itch continued and felt worse and worse like a worm was crawling up his spine, beneath his skin. He wanted more than anything to get it out.

"I hate that worm," he mumbled to himself, pulling out the knife from his pocket. "Always knew I'd have to cut it out myself."

The doctors stood, watching him. Making no effort to stop him from harming himself.

And so he did. As their blank faces observed him, he gripped the knife in his right hand. Holding it firmly, he lifted it up towards the back of his neck and began to cut. The men in white coats continued taking notes.

Something that he didn't recognize at first as pain, but a strange sensation like heat, began to emanate from that place, getting worse and worse, hotter and hotter, until he could stand it no longer and pulled the knife away. Then he reached up with his purple-bloodied hand and began to dig with his fingernails beneath the skin, digging for the worm.

Finally, he found it. The thing was tenacious, wrapped around him in places and coiled like a hard wire bent with pliers. Gritting his teeth in agony, he began to unravel it.

He looked up again as he was doing this and saw he was no longer surrounded by doctors, but by the dead. They were looking at him as if judging him, dozens and dozens all around, their forms grey and devoid of detail, as if made from smoke and shadows. He tried to ignore them and worked on the task at hand, unravelling the coiled metal which was wrapped around his insides, holding the malicious little worm in place.

It squirmed and wriggled beneath his skin, trying to get away, but finally he had it and pulled it out, long tendrils of bloody string stretching out behind it as he yanked it free and threw it to the ground, stomping it beneath his feet as hard as he could as it tried to scurry away.

Escape from the Asylum / Jordan Grupe

As he gasped and breathed heavily, the visions slowly started to clear. He could now see that he was in between two giant shelves filled with boxes. He was still in the warehouse and the sound of an argument was going on behind him.

"Gertrude, get down here! I need your assistance!"

He realized it was Mertzek shouting. The doctor didn't sound happy.

"I can't let you do this, Doc. Sorry, but I'm not going to let you poison the whole town. I'll shoot you if I have to."

"And go to jail," the doctor replied smoothly. "My boy, you don't want to go to a place like that. Trust me, you'll understand soon. Just like everyone else. This is for the best."

It dawned on Reynard that Gertrude was still preoccupied with Dell and he momentarily had the upper hand on the doctor, hidden as he was. He looked up quickly to see Gertrude was tying Dell up in the foreman's booth overlooking the warehouse, while Mertzek was in the middle of a standoff with Jordan, the security guard who he had given his gun to.

He realized he would be in quite a bit of trouble later on, when he filled out the report saying what happened there. Giving away your service pistol was not exactly standard operating procedure. But that was a problem for another day.

Reynard began to creep along behind the shelves, trying to make his way towards Mertzek who would still believe him incapacitated by the medication. Not that he wasn't feeling it still, but he was at least able to walk. The pain in his neck was excruciating, but at least his mind was finally starting to clear, he thought numbly.

He shifted off balance and tumbled into a stack of boxes on a nearby shelf. They went flying everywhere making a loud noise and Mertzek turned his attention back to Reynard's direction for a moment.

"Detective, is that you? I wonder what visions you're seeing this time... Hopefully they're talking some sense into you. Making you see the other side of things."

Reynard kept moving, his feet clumsy and his legs feeling wooden and stilted.

They had the upper hand. He just had to get behind Mertzek and...

"Oh, shit!"

The security guard called out in surprise from behind him but he wasn't able to see what had happened to elicit that reaction. Something told him that he needed to hurry, though. Whatever had just happened wasn't going to be good.

He came around the corner and saw Mertzek's eyes widen in surprise. Warm blood was still trickling down Reynard's neck and the pain was making his vision double, but still he stumbled forward and charged like a bull. The doctor was not expecting it.

Reynard crashed into him with the force of all his body weight, knocking the wind out of the man and sending him to the ground. He gasped for breath and Reynard couldn't help but relish the look of discomfort and unease on the doctor's face.

But then his eyes looked behind Reynard and he smiled infuriatingly.

He followed the doctor's gaze and saw Gertrude had snuck up on the security guard and was wrestling Reynard's gun from him. The guard was laying on the ground and was clearly being outmatched by the smaller opponent who was straddling him and holding his dominant hand in both of hers.

The gun eventually flew from his grip as she used a stress position to cause him to release it. Her military training was showing again as the guard made every effort to buck her off of him but was unable to do so.

Reynard had no choice. He stood up and raced over towards the woman as she put the security guard into a choke hold and began to squeeze.

Jordan's face turned pink, then red, then purple as he looked to be running out of air.

"I'll kill him," she hissed, as Reynard bent down and picked up his gun. "Don't touch it!"

But it was too late. He had the gun in his hand and despite her efforts she was unable to do any further damage before Reynard had his pistol aimed squarely at her face.

"Let him go. I swear to God I'll pull this trigger."

Her eyes shifted over his shoulder and he nearly looked there himself, wondering what the doctor was doing. But then he heard the sound of the door open and close and knew. The coward was running.

Reluctantly, she released him, and the guard began to huff and puff with grateful breaths of air.

"Good luck proving anything," she said, raising her hands in the air. "As far as anyone knows, I'm Allison. She's got the face tattoo, remember? She's the crazy one. You thought so yourself. Remember when we talked, Detective? You had no idea who I was, what I was capable of. We all wear masks. Only some of us wear them better than others."

He had to stop himself from laughing out loud. She couldn't have given him a better confession, especially after what the doctor had told them earlier. But he waited until she was in handcuffs to say anything.

"Actually, Gertrude," he said, after locking her wrists up tightly, pulling the phone out from the breast pocket of his jacket. The red "record" symbol was engaged, counting the minutes since the start of the raid. "I've got all the proof I need, right here."

Escape from the Asylum / Jordan Grupe

28: It's Always Darkest Before Dawn

After getting Dell untied from where he was up in the foreman's booth, the three of them took Gertrude outside, hoping that Philip had been able to stop Mertzek from escaping.

Unfortunately, they found the guard unconscious, laying on the ground. The doctor's black BMW was gone as well.

Philip began to rouse as they approached and when he was able to speak he told them he'd tried his best, but that the doctor was a lot tougher than he looked. And he'd had some sort of hypodermic needle with him as well, which he'd injected into Philip's neck, knocking him out for a few minutes.

"It looked like one of those injection guns from a spy movie or something," he explained. "I didn't even see it coming."

The four of them stood there with Gertrude awkwardly waiting, trying to decide on a plan.

"I know where he's going," she said suddenly. "I'll take you there, but only if you let me go."

Reynard laughed.

"Not gonna happen. You killed that guard at the mental hospital. You think we didn't know it was you? You tried to pin it on your sister, but you got sloppy. For one thing, she can't fight the way you can. And for another - the two of you have different fingerprints. You're gonna go to prison for a long time for that murder. Either that, or you're gonna go to the same place where they locked up your sister. Isn't that ironic?"

She stared at him with hateful eyes, but there was something else in them too.

"That's where they went, isn't it," Jordan asked. "Century Manor."

Her face dropped with a sudden look of disappointment and surprised recognition. His years of reading people let him know that look meant the guard's guess was right.

"Dell, I don't think you're gonna like this plan but here's what we need to do," Reynard said quickly. "We need to act fast - Mertzek gets to those tunnels down in the sub basement and he's gonna be gone forever."

"So, what's your plan?"

"I want you and Philip to stay here and call for backup," said Reynard. "Show them the evidence. I'll send you the video from my phone and you can tell them all about Gertrude and Allison, the doctor and his plan to poison the city, you tell them everything and get them to believe it. Then tell them where we're going."

"Are you sure we can trust Snead with this? He's got it out for you now.."

"So call the chief of fucking police for all I care - if there's ever been a time to go over that son of a bitch's head, this is it."

"Alright… And what are you gonna do?"

"Me and my security guard friend here are gonna go track down Mertzek at Century Manor before he can get too far. Philip is gonna stay with you and back up your story. He's got an inside angle that they can't argue with since Allison is his aunt. Tell them whatever you have to, Philip, but make sure they understand who this is and what she's capable of."

"Got it," Philip said, nodding.

"So let me get this straight," Jordan said nervously. "You want me to go with you into Century Manor, probably back into the basement again, to track down a possessed, murdering psychopath armed with a hypodermic gun? And after I told you everything I went through last time I was down there?"

"Who else could show me the way? Come on, I need your help. We can't let this maniac get away with everything he's done. And it sounds like this ghost - Samantha, as you call her - who possessed him, she needs to be dealt with somehow too. You've dealt with those types of problems before. I need your help. And Dell, you'll send backup once the police arrive, correct?"

Dell nodded, already on the phone.

"Alright," Jordan eventually agreed, relenting. "Let's go get this sonofabitch."

They arrived outside Century Manor and stepped out of the car to hear crickets chirping all around in the early morning air. It was cold and windy, a storm blowing in and fat drops of rain just beginning to fall from above.

Reynard pulled his coat tighter around him, looking up at the imposing old mansion and feeling a chill run down his spine. As he looked up at the ancient building he thought he saw someone looking down at them from one of the upstairs windows, but it could have just been his imagination.

The doctor's car was parked outside haphazardly and the front door of the building was swinging open, making loud banging noises as it crashed wildly against the brick facade in the blowing gusts of wind.

Reynard and Jordan approached the front door cautiously, and the guard pulled out his big flashlight and turned it on, pointing it inside.

A sound of creaking boards came from upstairs and Reynard pointed upwards. The guard nodded and they slowly entered the mildew-smelling mansion.

Inside, the wallpaper was peeling and yellow, the floorboards rotten and missing in places. An old chandelier was covered in dust and hanging precariously above the entry foyer, looking like

Escape from the Asylum / Jordan Grupe

the chain it was suspended from could snap at any second. As if to confirm this, in the next room to the right, a bathtub had fallen through the ceiling at some point in the distant past, leaving its wreckage in the living room where shattered furniture and porcelain was scattered everywhere.

"It's just like it was before the fire," the guard murmured quietly. "I don't understand how it's possible."

A sound came from the basement now, a sound like laughter, or maybe crying, it was difficult to tell. It sounded like a small girl.

"Oh no, not this again. I don't wanna do this," the guard said, turning around and heading for the exit.

Reynard reached to grab him, but before he could, the door slammed shut with a loud bang, drenching the place in complete darkness. Jordan ran to it and tried to open it, pulling on the handle and slamming his shoulder into it desperately. It wouldn't open.

"Why did I agree to come here!? I almost died in this place…"

The sound of squeaking floorboards came from upstairs again. And the sound of a man's laughter.

"Mertzek. He's upstairs. He has to be," said Reynard. "You go down there and deal with her, I'll deal with Mertzek."

He could tell that the guard didn't like the idea, but it was too late. He was already heading up the stairs and going to confront the bastard who'd tried to ruin his life. More than anything else, he wanted to know why. Why him?

29: Time to Face Your Demons

Jordan stood at the top of the stairs, hesitating. There was no reason to go down to the basement, not really. He could just stay up on the main level.

Except that he knew he couldn't do that. For some reason beyond his understanding, he felt responsible for this mess. For not acting sooner. If he didn't put Samantha's ghost to rest now, who knew what other chaos she might cause?

He began to slowly descend the staircase, heading into the basement, unsure of what he was going to do once he saw her. The rotted wooden steps bent and creaked beneath his feet, illuminated only by the meager light of his depleted flashlight. It flickered occasionally and he cursed himself for not buying a fresh set of batteries for it recently.

Finally, he reached the bottom and had a momentary flashback to the year prior when he had stumbled across a young girl and her father in this very basement, hacking a body into pieces with a saw while the little girl laughed.

His legs shaking with each step, he came out into that same large, open area. A utility room by the looks of it, at least once upon a time. His flashlight beam shone around the open space, showing bubbling, sagging wallpaper, the ceiling drooping down precariously in places and looking like it could cave in at any second.

Exactly how he remembered it - as if the place had never burned down. As if it had stood for a hundred and fifty years without interruption.

But he knew better.

And if the girl who brought this place back from the ashes could do something like that, she could certainly replicate the sound of squeaking floorboards from the second floor, and the sound of a man's voice - making it seem as if there was someone up there when really there was no one.

From behind him came the sound of a soft footstep, but by the time he turned around it was already too late.

Just as the hairs stood up on the back of his neck in recognition of what was happening, he felt a pinch in his neck, like a bee had just stung him.

"What the fuck," he managed to mumble, and tried to grab hold of his attacker. But by the time he had turned around the old man had slunk back into the shadows, scuttling away quietly and snickering to himself.

"Our friend is back," said Samantha from the other end of the room. "Can I play surgeon this time, daddy? Can I?"

She had not been there a moment ago, but now her form was solid and tangible, impossible to ignore.

"Oh, I think that can be arranged," said a voice from behind him, and he spun around to see the door leading back upstairs was now blocked by a solid-looking man who should have likewise been a ghost.

"Doug?? How? This isn't possible. You're fucking dead!"

All the ghosts from his past were suddenly appearing before him in this dark, cobweb-festooned basement. The terror that invoked made him forget all about the sting of the hypodermic device still planted in his neck, feeding poison to his brain.

Doug, his old security guard colleague, took a step toward him, his pudgy face breaking out in a crooked grin. His teeth were black and rotten, his mouth full of grave soil, spilling out while he spoke, worms and maggots tumbling with it.

Escape from the Asylum / Jordan Grupe

"Anything is possible now, Jordan. Let us show you the way. The way down into the darkness."

Reynard crept slowly up the old, rotten wood staircase. His flashlight illuminated the corridor at the top very well, a bright cone of light spreading outwards from its tip. His gun drawn, he crested the top and went towards the first door on the left. The place where he believed he had heard the noise.

He threw open the door, letting it bang against the wall to show there was no one behind it. Then he stepped in slowly and turned sharply to the left, pointing his gun at the air where nobody stood waiting.

It was strange, he had been sure of the sound of footsteps coming from this room. But now there was nobody here.

A titter of laughter came from behind him suddenly, the sound of a little girl running past the room outside, giggling playfully. He spun around as the hairs stood up on the back of his neck and goosebumps broke out over his skin everywhere.

You're changed now, he thought to himself. *Others would need the doctor's special cocktail to see these things, but not you. You've seen the other side. A gateway has already opened in your mind. This is your life now.*

He tried to wish away these thoughts but found himself unable to.

Exiting the empty bedroom, he went back out into the hallway, half-expecting to see a ghost or a little girl or both in one. But instead he saw nothing.

The door to the next room had been closed before, but now it was hanging slightly ajar. Reynard approached it slowly and went to open it. His gun was held up in his hand as he pushed the door open and looked inside.

Strangely, there was a woman standing there. She was facing away from him and wearing scrubs like a nurse. Her hair was long, matted, and dirty-white.

"Miss, are you alright," he asked cautiously. This could be a trick, but it also just looked like a nurse from the hospital had been kidnapped by the doctor and locked in this room. Had she been the source of the sound of footsteps creaking on the floorboards which he'd heard from below?

He walked over towards her slowly, keeping his distance. She stood totally still, facing the wall away from him.

"Whatever he did to you, you're safe now. Just come with me. It's alright."

But something told him it was not alright.

Gulping down a dry lump in his throat, he moved around her, trying to glimpse her face. He moved around her in a circle, wide enough so that she wouldn't be able to reach him. For some reason it felt to him like that was important, at least it was for now, that he kept his distance until he could see her face and know she was real.

And yet no matter how far he went around her, it was like the white, tangled hair covered her face completely on all sides. His blood went cold at this realization, and the woman with no face turned to look at him.

The wooden door slammed shut behind him and the sound of a girl's tittering laughter could be heard muffled through it from the other side.

He looked around the room and saw the drawings everywhere in blood, symbols and horrible scenes of violence, childlike and crude. Writing in strange, unrecognizable languages, symbols and hieroglyphs.

The woman with white hair covering her face cocked her head, considering him through the strands, he could just barely see her jet-black eyes.

"My daughter needs more paint for her pictures," she croaked in a wet-sounding voice. "Isn't she talented?"

"Fuck no, fuck no. Not again with this shit. I thought this was over. This is a nightmare. Wake up, wake up," Jordan was saying aloud, pinching himself and then slapping himself hard across the face.

Every breath he took of the rancid basement air made him want to vomit.

"You're right, this is a nightmare, a living nightmare, which you'll endure for the rest of your days. You took my life from me, took my wife and child from me," the dead security guard said, holding the hacksaw in his hand and taking another step towards him. "Where'd you go, Samantha? Don't you still want to play surgeon?"

The little girl was suddenly gone from behind him and he guessed that even she had her limitations. Her attention was being split between here in the basement and the detective on the second floor. His mind had brief lucid moments before flipping back into utter terror, and this was one such second where he recognized his situation.

"Help! Detective Reynard! I need your help!"

He screamed as the pudgy guard came towards him, his skin looking puckered, wet and grey, flesh missing in places. His grotesque smile stretched wider as he raised the hacksaw and tried to grab hold of him with his waterlogged hands, gravesoil black beneath the fingernails.

"There you are, my dear. Oh good, you brought the rope."

He spun around to see the little girl standing behind him, smiling and holding a long length of rope. Clenched between her teeth was the rustiest-looking scalpel he had ever seen.

And then, without any warning, the world went black as something hit him hard on the back of the head, causing him to fall like a ragdoll to the floor.

He had one last strange thought before losing consciousness.

They're real. The fucking ghosts are real. And they're gonna kill me.

Reynard heard the screams for help coming from the basement and immediately forgot about his own safety. A paternal instinct kicked in that he hadn't known he'd had.

I brought that poor kid here and sent him alone, unarmed, into the basement. Who the hell knows what he's running into down there?

But there was still the issue of the ghost woman holding the knife and moving towards him with it slowly from the center of the room. Except, she wasn't a ghost. Not anymore. Somehow she'd been brought back, made tangible and real again.

And real people could be hurt. They could be killed.

He raised his gun and fired at where her face should have been, behind the white hair. It struck true, and she hissed with pain but kept coming forward somehow, a red stain spreading outward from where the bullet had impacted her. She moaned with what might have been either pain or pleasure - it was difficult to tell.

"Fuck this," he said, frustrated and feeling short on time. He was worried about Jordan down in the basement.

This was beginning to feel more and more like a trap to separate the two of them. How could he have been so stupid?

With the benefit of his countless hours of practice at the gun range, he shifted the target of his pistol at the last possible second and pointed it at her hand which gripped the knife.

He would only get one chance, he knew, and he focused intently on his aim, praying the bullet would strike true.

Just as she was winding up to swing the knife at him, he shot her hand cleanly with the gun.

The sound of the shots were deafening in the confined quarters of the room, and his ears rang and stung with pain from the sound. But at least the knife was knocked free from her bloodied, disfigured hand as she recoiled in agony.

She screamed in a high-pitched wail as she held up her hand, now missing fingers and jetting black blood.

Reynard sensed his opportunity and shoved her towards the only window in the room, which cracked with the weight of impact.

Then he kicked her square in the chest and sent her flying through it as the window shattered to pieces.

She flew out onto the roof and tried to grab hold of something to stop herself from falling, her fingers scraping and skidding off the roof tiles and sending broken pieces flying as she screamed.

She fell from the roof and the wet sound of her impact from far below indicated her demise.

Well, that's gonna be some interesting paperwork to fill out, Reynard thought to himself.

He popped the magazine to check how many bullets were left and nodded to himself, satisfied. If he was lucky, he'd only need one.

"I'm coming for you, Mertzek. And you're not gonna get away this time."

Escape from the Asylum / Jordan Grupe

30: A Stitch in Time

Reynard went slowly down the old wooden stairs, sticking to the outside edges in order to keep the boards from creaking beneath his feet.

The basement was completely pitch black, illuminated only by the intense glow of his flashlight beam, leaving whatever it didn't touch in eerie darkness. A multitude of dust motes were floating in the air as he moved down towards the bottom step. The landing area at the base of the stairs was dank and moldy-smelling, walls lined with old chests and wardrobes whose doors were smashed and broken by urban exploring teenagers over the years. Graffiti covered the black mold-spotted walls from various decades in the past, ranging in colours and subject matter from the crude to the absurd.

A sound of muffled cries came from ahead, as if someone was trying to scream but they were gagged and unable to do so.

His Glock was raised and gripped firmly in both hands as Reynard stepped onto the waterlogged floorboards of the lower level. The old house seemed to sigh and breathe in and out as if alive as he drew nearer to his goal. He wondered if the hallucinogenic drugs the doctor had fed him were out of his system yet, or whether he was still suffering from the effects of the mind-altering homebrewed medications.

Above him, the ceiling looked unstable and bulged downwards precariously, appearing water-damaged and in severe disrepair. Again, it seemed to heave in and out in rasping, labored breaths, each one sounding like the wind whistling on the eaves during a storm. It looked as if the whole place could collapse at any second, burying them all alive down there. The thought of that terrified him and made him want to run, but he knew he couldn't. He owed the guard that much.

There was an enormous open room to the left through a doorway and he heard the muffled cries coming from that direction once again. Whoever it was, they were terrified, and nobody was stopping them from making noise, as if they wanted to draw him in. It sounded like the security guard.

As he looked inside, he saw that it was. The young man was tied to a chair at the far end of the room, thrashing wildly against his bonds as if being tormented by unseen captors. A trail of blood was running down his cheek, blooming with blood as it opened up, as if an invisible knife were tracing a line down his face, cutting as it went.

What have I done, he thought to himself. *The doctor is always a step ahead. I can't just walk into his trap. He's waiting for me.*

Reynard tried desperately to think of what else to do. Different options ran through his mind - he could stall for time, he could try to negotiate, he could retreat, or he could always go charging in like an idiot. Those last two options sounded like the worst ones so he considered the other two instead.

Stalling for time could get the kid murdered. So it was down to negotiation.

Here goes nothing...

"Mertzek, I know you're in there! The house is surrounded. It's over! Give yourself up!"

He refused to enter that big empty room. It was too large and dark and full of places to hide. The sound of the guard's whimpering cries rose in pitch and intensity as his voice gave way to a scream - a scream strangled by an old sock stuffed into his mouth.

"Leave the kid alone, Mertzek! He hasn't done anything to you! He doesn't deserve this!"

Another strangled cry, this one cut short. Reynard was surprised to see the hazy shape of two figures standing behind the security guard. A short, pudgy man and what looked like a young girl - their features obscured by shadows.

Reynard suspected who the young girl might be, but he wasn't sure about the man. It wasn't Mertzek, though, his voice was coming from somewhere else, and his silhouette looked nothing like the one he saw.

"Oh, Detective, you still don't understand. It isn't me torturing the poor boy. It's his own demons," said a voice from the shadows, much closer than he felt comfortable with.

The sonofabitch can't help but gloat.

"There's one thing I don't understand, Doctor Mertzek. If you'll indulge my curiosity."

Silence. Curious, uninterrupted silence.

"Why did you choose me for this experiment? That's the one thing I couldn't figure out. But then I had a dream. When you had me locked up, this was, but I didn't figure out the meaning of it until now. I dreamt that I was back in the hospital again, visiting my mother. She was surrounded by doctors in white coats, their faces all blank and expressionless. Unrecognizable - except for one. *You. How old were you back then, Doctor? And why did I remember your face so clearly, among all the others?"*

Silence continued.

"I tried so hard to remember anything from back then. And then just now it hit me. My father launched a complaint against one of the residents. A cocky, tall, young know-it-all resident who decided to prescribe my mother some new experimental treatment. A powerful electroshock therapy using higher voltage than had been prescribed previously. They kept most of it from me, but I overheard a bit. And my memory is good, doctor, especially when I start recalling something vividly like that. You killed her with that experimental treatment, didn't you? Did you just want to impress your bosses? Either way, I don't think they took kindly to your dangerous methods, did they?"

He waited for the doctor's response, hoping maybe it was working, that just maybe he was making him angry enough to give away his location.

Instead, the doctor tittered from the shadows, still hidden, his shadow-cloaked accomplices now disappeared into the darkness again as well.

"You're the one who complained, Reynard. You whined and complained that she wasn't acting the same anymore, and your father eventually agreed with you. Despite being just a boy, you nearly ruined my career. Just as I've ruined yours now."

"So that's it. This really is all about revenge for you. I'm glad the SWAT team will be busting in here any second. You deserve life in prison for what you've done, Mertzek. And for what you planned to do. Just give yourself up, it will be better for you if you do."

"You'll have to do better than that, Detective. I'm not quite as foolish as you are. I know the police aren't here. I know you're bluffing. This is all a private crusade by a disgraced Detective. You don't even have a badge anymore, I checked!"

Just as he said that the windows began to glare intermittently red and blue at their edges, around the outside of boards covering them. The sound of sirens wailing could be heard from through the brick and glass as it filtered down into the basement. The darkness was suddenly not so dark anymore.

"You told me you convinced his boss he was insane," an angry girl's voice whispered from the shadows. "That he wouldn't believe a word of his story!"

Reynard felt a shiver down his spine, this time not from terror, but triumph, his skin breaking out in goosebumps as he thought about his friends outside, coming to save him.

"See, that's what you don't understand, Mertzek. Because you've never had friends, have you? People who believe in you and trust you, no matter what happens. Family, Mertzek. Ever heard of it? Not a housekeeper who cleans and makes dinner for you, or subjects who you kidnap, but a real family. Friends who you can count on. You've never had anyone like that, have you? Because you think you're better than anyone who needs those things. Well, guess what, we're the ones who are gonna win in the end. Because we've got each other's backs!"

With that, the door upstairs broke in with a loud bang and the sounds of several others coming down to save him echoed through the house.

"He's down here," Reynard shouted, finally spotting Mertzek in the beam of his flashlight, trying to slink into the shadows and escape - probably through some hidden tunnel he had scouted ahead of time.

"Take one more step and I'll shoot you, Doc. Don't think I won't."

The old, white haired man raised his hands, just as Lieutenant Snead came down the stairs with Philip and Dell trailing behind.

"Lieutenant Snead! I'm so glad you're here," Mertzek shouted, his face red and flushed. "Please, you have to help me! This maniac has been harassing me, chasing me all over town! I hid in this abandoned building, thinking he wouldn't find me, but he chased me in here as well! Threatened to kill me!"

Snead had a pair of handcuffs with him and he walked over to Reynard, looking as if he was about to arrest him. His heart hammered with sudden panic, unsure if Philip and Dell had convinced him of the truth, or even if he could be convinced.

Mertzek had all kinds of tricks up his sleeve. Had brainwashing Snead been one of them?

He opened up the cuffs and hesitated, looking at Reynard with an eyebrow raised.

"Are you gonna arrest this sonofabitch or are you gonna make me do it for you?"

A whole team of policemen and women now had their guns pointed at Mertzek, ensuring he wasn't going anywhere. In the bright lights the ghosts had fled as well, he noticed.

"Franklin Reynard," Snead said, handing him his badge and gun. "I hereby reinstate you to your position as Detective. Now, please, arrest that man for aiding and abetting a murderer. We'll get to the conspiracy to poison the entire town later on. That'll work for now to get him off the street. I enjoyed your little film project, by the way. Although the camerawork was a little shaky."

Mertzek stumbled backwards, slipping and falling to the ground and in the process dropping the hypodermic gun which was tucked into his belt.

"No, no, no! He's insane! You all saw him! He's lost his mind. You can't believe what he's telling you - it's all lies!"

Reynard flipped the doctor over and brought his hands behind his back while he cried out pitifully in pain.

"OW! He's hurting meeeee!! Stop him! Why aren't you stopping him!?"

Snead picked up the hypodermic gun with the tip of his pen, keeping the fingerprints intact. He slid it carefully into a plastic evidence bag.

"Don't forget to read him his rights, Reynard. I don't want this man to have any legal recourse to get out of the punishment he so rightly deserves. Life in prison, I'd guess. Poisoning people, kidnapping, plotting to tamper with the town's water supply... That last one will get you more time than you'd imagine, doc."

Reynard read the man his rights, enjoying every second of it.

It was finally over.

Or so he thought.

Escape from the Asylum / Jordan Grupe

After The Storm

Suspect Interview: Dr. Werner Mertzek PhD
Inmate # 908020
Case: 4782-H264

Detective Flanders: Thank you for speaking to me today, Doctor Mertzek. As previously stated anything you say here can be used against you in a court of law. Now, can you please describe in detail the events which occurred Tuesday, the seventeenth of last month? Just prior to your arrest at Century Manor.

Doctor Mertzek: Ah, no, I don't think so. As I've previously stated, I will not speak to you, or anyone for that matter, aside from Detective Franklin Reynard.

Detective Flanders: Unfortunately, Detective Reynard is unable to join us today. Or at any time in the near future. We will need to speak to you without his company.

Doctor Mertzek: You don't understand me. I will not speak to anyone unless it is Detective Reynard. Those are my terms. You can see to these terms or I'll continue to remain silent. Guard! I'm finished!

Detective Flanders: Detective Reynard is no longer with the police department. He and Detective Dell have moved on. I've reviewed their statements and the statements of everyone else involved. Now I just need yours. It's the last one on the list. Now, please. Indulge me. I can keep an open mind. This many people... It isn't possible that all of them were having some kind of shared delusion. I believe something outside of what we

Escape from the Asylum / Jordan Grupe

understand as reality must have occurred that night at Century Manor. So... What was it?

Doctor Mertzek: (Silence for several minutes) I'll relent. If you'll tell me something. What happened to the sisters? Where are Gertrude and Allison?

Detective Flanders: Alright, we'll trade. I'll tell you a little something in exchange for something from you. Deal?

Doctor Mertzek: *nods silently*

Detective Flanders: Gertrude confessed to everything after she found out about the recording. There wasn't much point denying it after that. She told us how after their fight a year ago she carved up her sister's face with a tattoo gun to make her look insane. Knocked her out cold beforehand, then acted like she was the one who got attacked. With Gertrude's history, all she had to do was pretend she was her sister and let Allison take the fall for everything. To make matters worse, Allison received blunt force head trauma from the attack, which affected her memory. She didn't even really remember who she was for several months and just went along with the story she was being fed. Her amnesia was overlooked by the police and later by prison medical staff and dismissed as an attempt to avoid questioning.

When Allison escaped the asylum Gertrude found out, so she went back and killed the guard, posing as her sister. She used a Sharpie to write Betrayed on her forehead, to match for the cameras. All just to make sure the police hunted Allison down and threw her back in the asylum. She wanted to keep her life so badly she would have done anything.

Doctor Mertzek: So Reynard really did figure it all out.

Detective Flanders: No, not quite. Allison came back with Greg, just before the standoff at the warehouse. One of the guards at the hospital was her nephew and he believed her story, and so did Reynard. Between the two of them they convinced Detective Dell and that's why he joined them in hunting you down.

Doctor Mertzek: So Allison gets to live happily ever after now while her sister gets locked up...

Detective Flanders: I wouldn't go that far. Her husband is dead, after all. Thanks to your partner in crime. How exactly did you team up with that woman?

Doctor Mertzek: She came in to visit her sister one day. In that instant, I saw her. I knew what had happened... You could say a little birdie whispered it in my ear. I suspected something already, but I put the pieces together when I saw the look on Allison's face. That resigned, hateful look of betrayal. And I knew what she had done. And I knew I needed Gertrude on my side for what I planned to do. Someone that cunning - I needed her.

Detective Flanders: Why don't you start from the beginning, Doctor? From the very beginning.

Doctor Mertzek: I won't blame you for not believing me, Detective. I really won't.

Detective Flanders: Try me.

Doctor Mertzek: Well, I suppose it all started one evening after my shift. I was walking past Century Manor, the old building at the back of the hospital grounds. That was when I heard a voice calling to me for help. The voice of a sad, desperate little girl - injured and in trouble. At least, that's what I thought she was at first...

Jordan Grupe / January 20th, 2022

Manor House
905-648-4797
www.manor-house-publishing.com